The Guinea Child

To my wife Ann

The
Guinea
Child

MAYNARD DAVIES

Published 2015

www.arimapublishing.co.uk

ISBN 978 1 84549 675 3

© Maynard Davies 2015

arima publishing
ASK House, Northgate Avenue
Bury St Edmunds, Suffolk IP32 6BB
t: (+44) 01284 700321

Contents

CHAPTER 1

A Fresh Start

It was 1804 and England was at war with Napoleon. In the small town of Himley, a factory was busy making brass buttons for the army and the navy; gun barrels were also made here. The main gun barrel was produced in Torduff's foundry in Himley; this foundry was noted for the quality and reliability of its gun barrels. The head of the firm was Elijah Torduff, a devout Methodist. He and his wife Charlotte both had an active part in the business, as did their two sons, Roderick and Daniel.

The younger son, Daniel, was very proud of the family business that produced the best guns in the Kingdom. He took great pride in his part in producing the finest gun barrels in the country and was very proud of the Torduff name and its reputation, and he was very proud to be part of the Torduff family. Daniel was his father's favourite and he repaid that by giving his father good service, loyalty and sound advice on business matters. Daniel went to work each day and produced something he was proud of and he had the satisfaction of knowing he had given his father a good day's work.

Roderick, however, was the favourite of his mother. He had been spoilt early in childhood, and now he enjoyed the pleasures of life: women, gambling and alcohol. If ever two brothers were opposites, these two brothers were. In looks, Roderick also favoured his mother's side: he was fair, blue-eyed and over six foot tall. He knew he was handsome and traded on this fact. Daniel was like his father: shorter in stature but with wide shoulders, strong arms and a dark complexion. This was the difference between the two brothers; one favoured the mother and the other the father.

Himley was built on a four-foot seam of coal, an abundance of iron ore and limestone, all ingredients which helped to produce the good quality iron that made the Torduff product an excellent one.

Making gun barrels was a fairly simple procedure but there was also an element of skill and knowledge. Roderick always rejected the knowledge he could have obtained in the foundry, but Daniel readily accepted all the guidance, advice and skill he could learn from the foundry workers. The simple operation of making gun barrels was dependent on a wooden pattern and sand. The first part of the procedure was to make an imprint in the sand by using the wooden pattern and this was done by people called 'moulders'. The sand was dampened to hold the shape; then hot iron was ladled through a channel into the mould. Within twenty-four hours it had set and you had a gun barrel. This was the basic way it was made so it was very important that the patterns for the gun barrels were kept clean and in good condition. After use, they were brushed off, then stood on end and kept dry.

Forty people worked in the foundry, starting at six o'clock in the morning and working until six o'clock at night: a twelve-hour day. They had a break for breakfast at nine o'clock and dinner at one o'clock. It was hot, hard work so they had one concession that they could have ale while working on the foundry floor. The firm provided an ale boy who fetched it from the local ale house and this kept the men going for the twelve hour shift. This was a concession that the foundry workers really needed as they lost so much perspiration, fluid which the ale replaced.

One of the jobs Roderick had, which was allotted by his father, was to keep account of all the patterns for making the gun barrels. There were many different patterns for all the different sizes of gun barrels and they were all numbered. So it was Roderick's responsibility to make sure the patterns were well looked after, cleaned and kept in a place of safety after the moulders had finished with them.

On one occasion, however, Roderick had collected up the patterns of the gun barrels and taken them into the yard to be brushed off and cleaned ready for the next use. However, it was five minutes to six and Roderick wanted to be at the local tavern by seven o'clock so he left the patterns in the yard. As always, he was more interested in the pleasures of life than in his work. He sped off to the family home, which stood nearby in the foundry's yard. The house was called Chimneys after its large ornate chimneys. His mother kept three or four servants in the house, which was elegantly furnished. She had taste and good breeding and ran the house very efficiently.

It was five to six and Roderick wanted to be away to enjoy the pleasures of life in the tavern. There were three inns in the town of Himley but Roderick's favourite was The Raven. It was a large inn, with bedrooms for hire, a large tap room and a large vault with rows of barrels containing different ales for sale: there was a good choice of light beer, bitter or porter. They also had a concert room where they employed local artists to sing and play instruments. In the concert room there was a table of food available, if you bought a tankard of beer you were entitled to free food. The food consisted of cooked pastries, black pudding, bread, sausages, brawn, boiled eggs and sliced ham, so you could eat at the same time as you were drinking. Of course, the price of the ale covered the price of the food. Roderick went to The Raven because it fulfilled all his requirements of good ale, good food and an abundance of attractive female company. He was well known at the inn and he knew the landlord, John Canton particularly well.

During the course of this particular evening, as he drank and ate, John Canton talked with him and explained that he was intending to emigrate and he was going to sell the inn. He asked if Roderick knew of anyone who might be interested in purchasing the inn, as he was going to Australia in search of a better life. Roderick shook his head; he did not know of anyone now but if he heard of anybody, he would tell them to get in touch with John.

As the evening wore on, Roderick had his fill of food and ale and, at twelve o'clock, he decided he had enough of both, so he made his way back to Chimneys. He let himself in and went to bed. Unfortunately, during the night a heavy downpour of rain started which carried on for four hours. As usual, the house staff woke at five o'clock and began work. The downstairs maids lit the fires, the cook prepared the breakfast; the family had breakfast at an early hour as this was a working house. Breakfast was served in the main kitchen, then they made their way to the foundry to start the day's toil.

Immediately, their father noticed that the patterns had been left out all night. He asked who had left them out and Roderick admitted it was him. His father angrily replied that they would now be useless as they were soaked and, even when they dried out, they would surely be warped and worth nothing, other than for morning sticks. He explained this would stop them from making gun barrels for at least three weeks while the pattern makers made new patterns. He strode off angrily back to the house, sat down with his head in his hands, and said he was cursed with an imbecile for a son.

Like all mothers, Charlotte tried to pacify her husband, saying it was an accident and a very foolish thing for Roderick to have done. But the old gun maker said he was having no more of this nonsense and Roderick must leave that same day and plough his own furrow with his own horses; in other words, it was time they parted and he must make his own way in life. In spite of his wife's pleading, Elijah instructed one of the maids to pack all Roderick's belongings and put them in the main hall. At the same time, he sent one of the servants down to the foundry to tell Mr Roderick he was wanted back in the main house immediately. The gun maker sat in his large Windsor chair in the kitchen, waiting for Roderick's return. He had made his mind up and there was no turning back.

When Roderick arrived, Elijah looked at him and said he could see no future for him in the gun making business as he had always worked under sufferance and so it was time they parted company and he should make his own way in the world. He wished him all good fortune but, as far as working in the foundry was concerned, he would never make a gun maker and so this part of his life was at an end and he must now go out to make his own fortune in life.

Roderick was now completely on his own and he realised, for the first time in his life, that it was a cold, unwelcoming world outside of his comfortable home and life. All this trouble was of his own making and only he could put it right. He wandered down the path leading to the village, taking his pack of belongings with him. He went to The Raven, where the landlord was sitting outside. He commented that Roderick was early; so Roderick sat down and poured out all his troubles to the innkeeper. The landlord asked him what he was going to do now but Roderick did not know how to reply to this other than saying he would have to make his own way in life with no assistance from his family.

The landlord said, 'Opportunity knocks very softly. You have come here this morning knowing of my plans and, if you have the funds, you can buy the inn. You enjoy this kind of life so you would be paid for your enjoyment!' He told Roderick he wanted six hundred guineas for the inn, lock, stock and barrel, which would give Roderick a good living. Roderick knew his mother had sufficient funds and, when the time was right and his father was in the foundry, he would go back to Chimneys and ask his mother for six hundred guineas.

Therefore, at an appropriate moment, he made his way back to Chimneys, making sure he entered discreetly, and went straight to the parlour where his mother was sitting at the table. He said to his mother he had come for some assistance and, if she was prepared help him, he wanted to buy The Raven which would give him a living.

He said, 'I don't think Father will have me back in the business and I think I can make a success of it.'

His mother looked at him like all mothers do when their children need help and it is forthcoming. 'Six hundred guineas,' she said, 'That's a lot of money but I suppose you may as well use it as I never will.'

She rose from the table, went upstairs to her bedroom and took from her strong box a leather bag with the six hundred guineas. She returned to the parlour and handed the bag to

Roderick, 'This is the six hundred guineas but this is the first and last time I will give you any money. This will help you on your new path in life, I wish you all good fortune.' He kissed her tenderly, put the money into his pocket and left the way he had entered.

He strode back the way he had come down the winding path to the village. He entered the inn where the landlord was sitting at the far table. Roderick said, 'I have the funds to buy the inn, so it only remains for the paperwork to be done.'

The landlord replied, 'We will need the assistance of a lawyer to turn the deeds of the inn and the three acres of land over to you. We can start the procedure today and then I can be on my way on the coach to London as soon as it is completed.'

In due course the lawyer arrived, the deal was completed, the documents signed, the money was passed over and the deeds exchanged. Roderick was now landlord of The Raven Inn.

Roderick enjoyed his new life as the landlord of The Raven: the hours suited, the ale and the food suited and the women even better. He thought he had found his vocation and enjoyed every minute; moreover, he was paid for something that he thoroughly enjoyed. The year went by and, by the time November came around, Roderick was settling into his role as host of the inn.

One night, when the snow had started to fall, a young woman entered the inn and asked his permission to make a collection amongst the customers to build a meetinghouse for the Quakers. Roderick looked at her, 'A meetinghouse for the Quakers?'

'Yes,' she replied, 'My father, mother and my two sisters are going to build a meetinghouse outside the village.' Roderick was struck by her innocence, her beauty and her courtesy; it was the first time in his life he wanted to be with a young lady who did not frequent the inn. In a bold manner he asked her name.

'Sarah Allen,' she replied.

'So, you want to build a meetinghouse for the Quakers?'

'Yes, Sir,' she answered.

He asked her how he could assist and she replied, 'If I could just ask your customers for a few pence contribution to build the meetinghouse, that would help greatly.'

He readily agreed to her collection as he wanted to make her acquaintance and intended to use the opportunity to do so and get to know her better. On several occasions she came into the inn to collect and he would stay in the main bar to watch her weaving her way between the customers with her collecting tin. Customers in the inn were a friendly crowd and they were also generous to Sarah and her cause.

On one occasion, Roderick decided he would have a word with Sarah Allen and ask if she would like to have a drive with him in the country with his new horse and trap. She looked at him, 'No, Sir, I could not do that because I do not agree with the business you are in, selling ale, whisky and drink to the people and I will not go into the country with you on any occasion.'

This was the first time in Roderick's life he had been turned down by a young lady, the only time in his life when he had met any opposition from the fairer sex. This dented his pride that a young lady had flatly refused his attentions and it made him more determined than ever to make her acquaintance.

On the next occasion Sarah arrived at the inn to collect money, Roderick was there, well presented, and he asked again.

'Would you consider one Sunday afternoon, a ride in the country in my horse and trap?'

She looked at him, 'Sir, I will repeat, I will not drive in the country with you.' She paused and then said, 'However, if you give up the drink, I will drive in the country with you, but I will bring my two sisters with me.'

This rather jolted Roderick because the answer had a sting in the tail and he wasn't having his own way. She told him he would have to ask her father if it was permissible and, if he agreed, she and her sisters would accompany him on a drive one Sunday. This bowled Roderick over completely, he had never come across this situation before. He had no alternative but to go and see Mr Allen to ask permission to take his daughters out one Sunday afternoon.

Accordingly, one morning he visited Quaker Allen to seek his permission to take his daughters for a drive. The old Quaker gave him a piercing look before answering but he then gave Roderick his permission to take his daughters out, as he thought they would enjoy that.

Roderick realised that to make any progress with Sarah he would have to adopt a better way of living. He gave up the demon drink and reformed his ways and both began to take something away from the occasions when they met. Roderick's health improved now that he was no longer drinking and Sarah gained a friend and a drive in the country each Sunday with her sisters.

As the relationship developed with Sarah, Roderick fell in love with her; this was something he'd always wanted. He grew to appreciate her innocence, honesty and beauty and fell deeply in love with her. It was the first time in his life he ever really understood that true love existed and he intended never to let it go. Whatever it was going to take, he was going to marry Sarah if at all possible. As time went on, the relationship developed and deepened and they came to love each other. They realised they had attained something in life that was very rare in that they were both suited to each other. She was a devout Christian and he was learning to become one and enjoying the experience. When he asked her to marry him, she told him he must ask her father's permission.

So, one morning, he went to see the old Quaker to ask his permission for his daughter's hand in marriage. The old Quaker said to Roderick, 'You are not the ideal husband I would want for Sarah. She is my favourite but I can see you are both in love and I will not stand in your way. I will give you my permission if you will become a Quaker and, when you marry, you must find another abode, a home for Sarah away from the inn. The inn is your business and you must run it but I want Sarah to have her own house and domain.' Roderick readily agreed to these conditions because his goal was to marry Sarah so the price could never be too great or too hard to obtain.

He decided to return to Chimneys and the foundry and ask his mother and father if they wished to come to the wedding. When he visited Chimneys, to ask his father and mother for their blessing, his father came in from the foundry and said to him, 'You have made good progress in life and have found something you like to do and I am proud of you.'

Sitting in her chair, his mother said, 'I understand you are going to marry Sarah Allen, the Quakers' daughter. I believe they are nice people and I hope you make her a good husband.'

'Yes, luck has shone on me and I will not let anyone down because all we seek is happiness,' Roderick replied.

His father asked about the arrangements for the wedding and Roderick told him he had not yet made any. The father looked at his son, 'Your mother and I have decided that we will provide a good wedding breakfast here at Chimneys. We also understand from Quaker Allen that you are to provide an alternative home other than the inn for Sarah.'

Roderick nodded his head then his mother said, 'As a gift to you, I will give you my family home, Cheswardine Hall, which is the other side of the village; there has always been much love in that house. We will bestow that to you as your wedding gift, as you are my first-born.' She continued, 'I want to give you a good start in life as your father and I had. It has been a stony road you have walked, for a long time, but I think you are walking a better road now, so we are going to give you Cheswardine Hall as a gift. I think you will find happiness there, as my family have done for many years.'

CHAPTER 2

A Quaker Wedding

The task of making the dress for the bride began. The Quaker women were good with their needles and the very simple yet beautiful dress began to take shape. Sarah's sisters would be her attendants and their dresses were duly made to complement the bride's.

Roderick's mother organised the wedding breakfast at Chimneys and chose the menu with the cook. It was to be a simple wedding breakfast as the Quakers lived a simple life. It was the custom in those days to have an organiser for weddings and, in the village of Himley, there was a lady called Mrs Winter who specialised in providing this service for weddings, funerals and christenings. Charlotte decided to engage her to organise the wedding and she sent her a note, requesting her to attend at Chimneys.

Mrs Winter duly arrived. She was a tall, thin woman and she was shown into the library where Charlotte was waiting for her. Charlotte and Mrs Winter discussed the wedding breakfast and Mrs Winter suggested that, as it was to be a non-alcoholic wedding, she suggested the drinks should be tea, chocolate and coffee, as was the custom of the day. She also suggested that they had a baron of beef, mutton legs, faggots, York ham, brawn and a variety of sweet meats, a variety of breads, butter, and, for the dessert, raspberry pie and gooseberry pie. This, together with a good selection of cheeses, should be sufficient. The wedding cake would be a very simple affair in deference to the Quakers. Mrs Winter said she would provide all the extra servants for the day and Miss Charlotte should provide all the crockery and glasses. Mrs Winter inspected the large dining room and discussed with Miss Charlotte the decorations and the flowers. Miss Charlotte thought Mrs Winter seemed a very competent lady and was glad this stage in the arrangements was completed.

The floral arrangements were discussed with the gardener and it was decided they would be simple in appearance as the Quaker wedding service is very simple. The meetinghouse would have wild flowers and the aisle would have rose petals scattered along its length.

The next step was to arrange to hire two white horses to pull the carriage to take the bride to the meetinghouse. The family enjoyed making these arrangements as preparing for a wedding is a joyful time. The wedding date was set for the second of May, the arrangements were on course and everyone was happy.

Roderick had decided to take Sarah to Cheswardine Hall, which had been a gift to them from his parents, so she could see her new home. He was wise enough to understand that women choose their homes and men live in them and so, on this basis, he asked Sarah if she would like to see Cheswardine Hall one afternoon and see if she would like to make it her home. She agreed once permission had been sought from her father for the excursion.

So, on the agreed afternoon, Roderick set off for the old Quaker's home. As he arrived at the door, Sarah came out and looked at the pony and trap.

'You have got a new pony and trap,' she said.

'No, I have not; this is your pony and trap. This is my gift to you, so you will be able to visit your family, if you choose to live at Cheswardine, as it is a little remote.'

Roderick had chosen well with the pony, he had a long mane and a long tail, he was black and white and was a pretty pony. Sarah was very taken with him and asked what his name was. Roderick told her she could name him so Sarah thought for a moment then said, 'I think I will name him Jess.'

Roderick helped her into the trap, saying, 'This is your pony, your trap, your reins,' and handed her the reins. They set off for Cheswardine Hall, knowing happiness was theirs and they were going to enjoy their life together.

Cheswardine Hall was about ten miles on the other side of the village and lay off the main road, down a lane, through a wooded glen and up a long drive. The house stood back from the drive. It was made of quarried stone, with two gabled ends, leaded light windows and a large lawn in front.

As the pony was trotting up the drive, they noticed smoke coming from one of the chimneys. This puzzled both of them, as the house had not been occupied for many years. As they arrived at the front entrance, they saw a man standing on the porch. Roderick and Sarah drew level with the entrance and the man stepped forward and took the horse's halter. Roderick stepped down and said, 'I have not had the pleasure of your acquaintance.'

The man replied, 'You may have forgotten Sir, but I remember when you were a little boy and you came here with Miss Charlotte Torduff to visit your grandfather. That was many years ago. My name is Abel I have been retained by your mother to look after Cheswardine.'

He explained to Roderick that he was born on the estate and had been at Cheswardine all his life. He said that he had received a message from Miss Charlotte that they were coming to Cheswardine today so he had lit a fire in the sitting room as a welcoming gesture.

Roderick said, 'I apologise to you, I did not recognise you but I remember you now.'

Abel said to Sarah, 'Would you like to look round Cheswardine?' Sarah replied she would indeed and would like to go carefully round one room at a time. Roderick and Abel stood in the hall but Sarah, like all women, was eager to explore the house and she went first into the dining room.

This was a long narrow room with a large mahogany table and twelve ladder-back chairs. On one wall of the dining room was a dumb waiter and on the other wall was an oak dresser with pewter plates. There was also a large fireplace, with brass tongs next to the grate. The floor was made of wide oak planks, well looked after and highly polished. All in all, Sarah thought it was a very comfortable room.

She then walked out of the dining room into the sitting room, where she found five high-backed leather chairs and another large fireplace with a big cast-iron grate. The walls were wood panelled with English oak and there was a large clock on the mantelpiece, which seemed to keep good time. There were pictures on the walls of hunting scenes and family portraits.

Sarah's next step was to cross the hall and go into the kitchen. It was a large kitchen with a big pine table in the middle. There was a pine dresser, laden with pots and pans and all the kitchen utensils. At the end of the kitchen, there was a cast iron cooking range and a door leading to the second kitchen, as was usual in big houses. The first kitchen was for cooking all the food and the second kitchen was used to prepare it.

Beyond the second kitchen was a long passage where the larders were, there were two larders: one for game and bacon and one for all dried goods, flour, rice and beans.

Sarah decided that she would like to see the bedrooms next and so she walked through into the hall where Roderick and Abel were still and said to Abel, 'I would like to inspect the bedrooms.'

Abel said, 'Certainly Miss Sarah, but would you like me first to tell you a little bit of the history of the house? A hundred years ago, there was a fire and half of the existing house was destroyed. The De Witts never rebuilt that part but that made it more manageable.' Abel then told them he would leave them to explore on their own and he hoped they would be very happy here and that they would enjoy the house.

Sarah and Roderick stood in the large hall and gazed around them, admiring the lovely old oak staircase. They continued to gaze around in wonder as they made their way up the staircase towards the bedrooms. The first bedroom they entered looked over the large lawn at the front of the house, this was obviously the master bedroom.

Sarah said to Roderick, 'Shall we have this bedroom for ourselves?' and Roderick replied, 'If that pleases you,' so the decision was made, this was to be their bedroom. There were another four bedrooms on the same floor and, on the top floor, there were four smaller bedrooms for the servants.

Sarah then wanted to look at the outbuildings, which were such an important part of farming so she went through the back entrance and found a large square farmyard.

She walked across the courtyard and found Abel who offered to show her round the buildings. The first building Sarah went into was the old dairy, which had not been in use for twenty-five years. Sarah asked Abel whether it was still workable and Abel said that everything was there, it just needed a good clean. A dairymaid would be able to make cheese and butter and this would bring it back to life. Sarah was impressed with the dairy and thought that, once cleaned and maintained, it could be a valuable asset.

Next to the dairy was a laundry with two huge cast-iron round boilers, which were all in good condition. All that was needed was for them to be cleaned out. Once cleaned and a fire lit, the laundry would soon be in good working order. There were still the hooks in the ceiling and the wires for holding the cotton sheets.

There were stables, which could house five horses, they were all mahogany lined and Sarah thought that Jess would enjoy having one of the loose boxes. Next to the stables was the brewing house which had not been used for many years but, when Sarah asked Abel if it was workable, he said, 'All the vats are still here and, given a good clean, it could be in operation within a week. When the estate was in good working order we hired a hundred and thirty men, and when it was harvest time we had a hundred and fifty men, and a brewing house was considered essential. This was when Cheswardine was a manor house.' Sarah was impressed with the farm buildings and she thought there was great potential.

Abel asked Sarah if she had enjoyed coming to Cheswardine and looking around the house and the buildings to which she replied, 'I've enjoyed it very much and I'm sure that Mr. Roderick and I could be very happy here.'

Abel said that it had always been a happy house but it had been asleep too long. He added, 'I am sure you will make this a happy home as it has lacked love and attention. I am sure a lady of your standing will wake the estate up.' Sarah said she had much enjoyed her visit to Cheswardine but that they should start to make their way back as it was getting late. She asked Abel to fetch the horse and trap around for them.

Abel replied, 'The lady and the gentleman of the house must leave by the front door. The second front door is for tradesmen and visitors; the farmyard is for horse traders and gypsies.' Sarah laughed and asked Abel whether he knew that they were getting married in a month, on May 2nd.

'There may be no newspapers in the countryside, but we do have storytellers and news carriers,' Abel replied, at which Sarah laughed.

She said to Abel, 'Could you arrange for the bedroom to be made ready and the kitchen to be in good working order. And now, if you bring the horse and trap around, we must leave.'

Abel said, 'That will be done, Miss Sarah, and I wish you much joy on your wedding day.'

Sarah climbed into the trap and took the reins as Roderick got in the other side. They made their way back up the long winding drive, heading for Sarah's home.

They arrived back at Quaker Allen's home and Sarah said to Roderick, 'Would you like to come in for a moment, and then I will take you back to the village?' Roderick went in with Sarah to a long room with a table in the centre, but with chairs hanging on the wall, as is traditional in the Quaker home.

Her father, Quaker Allen, said to Roderick, 'I believe you have been to Cheswardine?' and Roderick replied, 'Yes, I have not been there for a long time; it brought back many memories of when I was a little boy.'

Her father asked Sarah whether she liked Cheswardine and she said it was a lovely old house and that she thought they could be happy there. Quaker Allen was pleased to hear this and then added, 'Before I forget, there is a letter which came from Chimneys. I believe it is from Miss Charlotte.'

Quaker Allen passed the letter to Sarah who read it quickly and then explained to Roderick that it was from his mother, Miss Charlotte, and it was an invitation to go to Chimneys to discuss the wedding and the wedding breakfast. She asked Roderick if he would deliver her letter of acceptance of the invitation to his mother when he returned home.

The day came round when Sarah was to go to Chimneys and, whilst Sarah was dressing, her father offered to put Jess into harness. Sarah said to her father, 'That is a kind thought. Before I leave, could I go into the flower garden and pick a bunch of flowers to make a posy for Miss Charlotte?' to which her father readily agreed.

Sarah came down the stairs and asked her mother, 'Do I look presentable for my visit to Chimneys?'

Her mother replied, 'You do not need silver buttons or gold bangles, God gave you beauty; that is all you need.'

Sarah made her way with Jess through the lanes to Chimneys. Jess was in good spirits and pulled the gig very well. It was a lovely morning, a warm spring day with the first flush of green showing on the trees. Within half an hour she had arrived at Chimneys where the old iron gates were standing open for her. She drove the gig around to the front of the house and the main door opened. One of the young servants came down and greeted her, 'Good morning, Miss Sarah. Miss Charlotte is waiting for you and I will escort you to her.'

Sarah asked, 'Where will I leave Jess?'

The young man said, 'I will take the pony out of the shafts and leave him in the stables as I am sure you will be here a considerable time with Miss Charlotte.'

Sarah went through the front door into a large hall where Miss Charlotte was waiting for her; she greeted Sarah with a kiss on the cheek.

'Welcome to Chimneys. I have been looking forward to you coming and I want to make sure we can have a long talk about the wedding breakfast and any ideas we can both contribute to make it a success.'

Miss Charlotte led the way into the sitting room where a log fire was burning and a tray of tea was set for two. Miss Charlotte opened the conversation, 'I am very pleased you are marrying Roderick as he needs a good wife to calm him down. He has a wild streak and it will do him good to settle down. I believe you will be a good wife to him and guide him along the path to a better way of life.'

Sarah felt somewhat ill at ease but replied, 'I hope you are right.'

Miss Charlotte continued, 'As you know, I have two sons, Roderick and Daniel, but I would have loved a daughter and I hope you can become my daughter and that we can become good friends.' Sarah told her she hoped also that they could become good friends and have a good relationship, because this would be in everyone's best interests.

Miss Charlotte explained to Sarah what she had discussed with Mrs Winter, the wedding organiser. They discussed the menu for the wedding breakfast and agreed there would be roast beef, mutton legs and many savoury dishes and of course no alcohol, only tea, coffee and chocolate. Miss Charlotte asked whether Sarah and Quaker Allen would object if they had a fiddler at the wedding as it would make the atmosphere very congenial and everyone would enjoy the music. She pointed out that there was a fiddler in the village that would be available.

Sarah thought this was a good idea and could see there would be no objections from her father or mother.

Sarah and Miss Charlotte were quickly building a very good rapport which was a bonus for everybody because sometimes in life that does not happen and problems can result. The discussions continued with arrangements for the wedding breakfast until the menu was finalised, the fiddler was agreed and the time of the wedding at the meetinghouse was confirmed. Both felt comfortable with the arrangements and were looking forward to the joyous day.

Miss Charlotte said to Sarah, 'I believe you went to Cheswardine and you met Abel?' Sarah replied that she had. Miss Charlotte told her that Abel was born on the estate and she had kept him on to look after the estate. She asked Sarah if she felt comfortable there and Sarah told her she felt very comfortable at Cheswardine and she was sure she and Roderick would be very happy there.

Miss Charlotte replied, 'I very much hope so as Cheswardine was my family home and, as you know, I am the last of the De Witts. I never wanted to sell it as the house holds so many memories, mostly happy memories. It is very run down as my father died a very long time ago and unfortunately the estate has been neglected since, but I feel that you and Roderick between you can put new life into Cheswardine and the estate.'

Miss Charlotte continued, 'I would like to tell you a little bit about the history of the Hall. My family lived there for just over three hundred years. Originally, the estate used to produce wool for the cloth trade, it was then woven nearby and sent to London to be sold. The estate prospered but, as time went on, the wool trade declined and so the estate declined, and we never found another product as profitable as wool.

'There are many possibilities with Cheswardine, there is woodland which has large oaks; these need thinning and the oak will fetch a good price. The house is well built even though it is only half the size that it was, but that could be an advantage. All the ingredients for a successful estate are there but it just needs some care.

'When I married Mr Torduff, people in the county said, in marrying a gun maker, I had married down but, in my opinion, I had married up. Torduff's foundry produced one of the finest products in England, the gun barrels, and we provided employment for the local people and we felt we had made our way well in life together. So, this has been my life, Sarah, and I hope, when you and Roderick go to Cheswardine, you put a lot more life into it than it has had for many years.'

As the meeting went on, the atmosphere relaxed and, the more they stayed in each other's company, the more they respected each other. They had a wonderful ingredient between them, they were honest with each other, which is always the ingredient which makes people comfortable together. Sarah knew she would get on with Miss Charlotte, and Miss Charlotte felt the same.

The afternoon wore on and dusk started to fall. Miss Charlotte told Sarah she must come and visit again and Sarah replied, 'That is very kind, I would enjoy that.'

Miss Charlotte rang for the manservant and told him to make ready the trap. He harnessed Jess, lit the oil lamps, and led Jess to the front door. Miss Charlotte escorted Sarah to the cart and Sarah climbed onto the cart, bade farewell to Miss Charlotte, and set off on her journey home to the other side of the village.

As she reached the gate, she turned and waved, Miss Charlotte waved back, and Sarah knew she had a mother-in-law, but she also knew she had made a friend.

Sarah told Roderick that she was going to put a notice in the Quaker house that they intended to marry. It was customary to post this notice on the door of the prayer house one month prior to the date of the wedding. Quaker marriages are a little different from other religions in that the bride and the groom make a simple statement to each other. In this case Roderick would say, 'I take Sarah my friend as my wife,' and Sarah would say, 'I take Roderick my friend as my husband.' The ceremony is that simple although sometimes rings are exchanged too. Once the words have been spoken, they would then sit down together. Sometimes an elder Quaker would give a sermon but not in all cases. The Quaker marriage was a very simple affair. Sarah posted the notice that in one month's time, the wedding would take place.

The remaining month passed quickly and May 2nd arrived. As for all weddings, everyone in the house arose early. Sarah's mother arose particularly early to start preparations as she had two other daughters to attend to and make sure they were well presented. Sarah arose and dressed herself with some assistance from her mother and sisters. She wore a very simple dress which was cream coloured and, in her hair, she wore a ringlet of flowers which had been gathered by her sisters that morning. She looked beautiful and radiance shone from her. Sarah's mother and sisters were dressed in the traditional Quaker clothes. Quaker Allen was also in traditional Quaker dress and was a little nervous. The horse and carriage was booked for nine o'clock and the wedding was to take place at half past ten. The old Quaker gathered all his family together, they said a prayer for Sarah, and all wished Sarah good fortune, much happiness and a long life, as was the Quaker tradition.

The horse and carriage arrived promptly at nine o'clock. The horses were York coaching horses which were the ideal horses to pull the carriage as they had a high step and fitted the part perfectly. Quaker Allen asked Sarah if she wanted him to sit in the carriage with her or whether she wanted him to walk with her mother and sisters. She replied, 'No, Father, I would like you to sit in the carriage with me as it would give me more confidence. I do feel a little nervous.'

Before Sarah stepped into the carriage, she went up to her mother, put her arms around her and said, 'Thank you for everything, Mother. You have been wonderful to me.'

Her mother looked at her and answered, 'You have fulfilled every happiness in life for me, I wish you great happiness, too. You will be greatly missed from here; it is a new life you are starting but I know you will be happy.'

Sarah asked, 'Do I look all right?' Her mother told her she looked wonderful and could not improve on how she looked. It was her special day and she should enjoy every moment, then she gave her a big hug and kiss, which spoke volumes.

Sarah stepped into the carriage followed by her father, the coachman flicked his whip and the horses set off. Sarah's mother, sisters and the rest of the Quakers followed on foot. Eventually they arrived at the Quaker meetinghouse where there was quite a large crowd to see the bride and some to attend the wedding. Roderick and his family had already arrived and were sitting on one side of the meetinghouse.

Roderick wore a blue velvet coat, a velvet pair of knee britches with silver buttons and a pair of high boots, a silk cravat and a silk shirt. He looked well presented; the difference between both families was well marked as Roderick's family were well dressed in fashionable clothes and the Quakers wore their plain simple clothes. Nobody could mistake from where both families had come.

Everyone was sitting on the plain simple forms, waiting for the ceremony to begin. As was custom, Roderick stood up and said, 'I take my friend Sarah as my wife.' Sarah stood up and repeated, 'I take my friend Roderick as my husband.' Sarah then walked across to Roderick and took his hand and they were married after this simple ceremony. Hand in hand, they walked back and sat on one of the benches. One of the elders then stood up and said to the couple, 'I wish you all happiness and I hope you are blessed with many children and an abundance of happiness. I speak for all the Quakers here in wishing you great joy and many years of happiness together.' The elder sat down, everyone bowed their heads in silent prayer and the ceremony was over.

Roderick stood up, took Sarah's hand and they made their way to the door, where the carriage was waiting outside. Roderick helped Sarah to board the carriage and they were followed by their parents as they all made their way to Chimneys for the wedding breakfast.

The carriage arrived at Chimneys where Charlotte had made a wonderful display of flowers on the steps of the house and all the servants were waiting in line at the foot of the steps. Sarah and Roderick alighted from the carriage and one of the maids gave her a beautiful bouquet of flowers and said, 'Welcome to Chimneys.' They walked into the main hall where a fiddler and a flute player were waiting and, as they walked on into the dining hall, the fiddler and the flute player preceded them, playing a fine tune. Everything blended well, they had good food, good company and good music: it was the start of a good life.

As the guests arrived at the house, Roderick's father and mother welcomed them all. Sarah and Roderick stood at their sides and welcomed the Quakers as they came into Chimneys and introduced her sisters to them. Then came the rest of Roderick's family and everyone was introduced to each other, and the party with the fiddlers and the flute player got off to a good start.

Soon everyone was drinking and having a good time. All the food was laid out in the dining room on the long table and everyone helped themselves, as was traditional at a wedding breakfast. Miss Charlotte had organised an excellent wedding breakfast and there was plenty to eat and drink. After everyone had had their fill, the fiddler called out that it was time to start the reels, so he and the flute player stood in the middle of the room and played, and the festivities began.

Everyone began to relax and enjoy themselves. They started to realise that, no matter how different their lives, they all liked to have a good time and they all lived in the same world. As the afternoon went on, some of the guests decided it was time to leave so they said their farewells, wished Roderick and Sarah many years of happiness and left, having thoroughly enjoyed the party.

Miss Charlotte called Roderick and Sarah to her and told them she would like to see them in the library. As they entered the room, they saw on the table a large mahogany box. Miss Charlotte said, 'I am going to give you this box and the contents, as I believe they belong to Cheswardine. I want you take this with you as you return to my family home. I would be grateful if you did not open it now but take it to Cheswardine . I hope you enjoy the gift.'

Roderick said to his Mother, 'I think it is time we made our way to Cheswardine. The pony Jess has been brought here to take us back and I think we should be making our way home.'

Miss Charlotte beckoned one of the male servants, 'Could

you please put this chest on Mr Roderick's cart.' It took two footmen to lift the chest as it was very heavy but it was finally loaded onto the cart.

Roderick stood in the middle of the room and thanked the remaining guests for coming, saying, 'I wish you all good fortune. My wife and I will now leave you to carry on enjoying yourselves. Thank you for your company and your good wishes.'

Roderick, Sarah, Quaker Allen and his wife and Roderick's parents all walked to the front door. Roderick helped Sarah onto the trap and then walked around to the other side. Someone had decorated the cart with flowers, even decorating Jess's harness so there was no mistaking it was a wedding cart. They set off on their way to Cheswardine and the start of their new life, with high hopes for a bright and happy future.

CHAPTER THREE

Awakening Cheswardine

It took about three quarters of an hour to get from Chimneys to Cheswardine. They pulled into the long drive, lovely trees lining either side of it. They could just see smoke curling from the two chimneys and Sarah and Roderick knew that Abel had kept to his promise and lit the fires. As they drew up to the porch, Abel was waiting there and he greeted them, 'Welcome to Cheswardine, your new home'.

They stepped down from the gig and Sarah said to Abel, 'Would you take the chest and put it in the library,' and Abel replied, 'I will, Miss Sarah'.

As they walked into the hall there was a warm atmosphere as the log fires had been lit earlier in the day. They went straight to the library and Abel followed them carrying the large chest, which he placed on the table.

Sarah could not wait to open the chest. In it, she found a letter and a small package and underneath this, there was a great quantity of silver cutlery. She opened the letter and read, 'To my dearest daughter-in-law, I feel this gift belongs at Cheswardine. It lived there for a long time and, as we do not entertain at Chimneys a great deal, I feel that it should return to its former home. I hope you enjoy using it and I hope that you will do so on many happy occasions.'

Sarah then picked up the small package and saw that attached to it was a note which said 'This is a gold locket which belonged to my mother and, as I have no daughters, I feel that you should have something which belongs to Roderick's family, as a welcoming gift.'

At that point, Abel came back into the room to ask if everything was satisfactory and Miss Sarah said she was pleased that the house felt warm and asked him how he had got on. He said that his wife Rose had come in and had made the master bedroom ready with clean linen sheets on the bed and had lit the bedroom fire for them. Sarah thanked him for this and then Roderick asked, 'Is Rose the same young lady that used to work for my mother?' and Abel replied, "Yes, my wife is the person you remember and she now lives with me in the cottage on the estate. She came in to prepare the master bedroom for you.' Abel then added, 'I wish you goodnight and I hope you enjoy living here at Cheswardine,' and took his leave.

Roderick asked Sarah if she would like to look around and see what changes had been made so far to the house. Sarah said she would and went straight from the library into the dining room then into the large kitchen. There she found everything had been thoroughly cleaned and given a new lease of life. They agreed that it now looked as though somebody lived there once again. Roderick said to Sarah, 'Well, it has been a long day, should we now go to bed?' and they made their way up the stairs together and walked into the master bedroom, which was on the first floor overlooking a large lawn.

Rose had done a good job in the master bedroom and there were clean linen sheets on the four-poster bed, with curtains on either side. With a roaring log fire in the grate, Sarah and Roderick settled down for the night and the start of their new life together.

The following morning, Sarah was up early to explore her new home. Men live in houses but women make a home: that is something that men do not understand but all women know. Sarah went all through the house, starting with the cellars, where she found the old wine store. It was empty and looked rather lonely with nothing on the shelves. She then visited the game store, which was next door and climbed the stairs to the back kitchen.

Cheswardine had two kitchens; a large kitchen where all the food was cooked and the servants took their meals and a back kitchen where all the vegetables and meats were prepared. There were two sets of stairs: the main stairs off the large hall and then the servants' stairs, which rose from the kitchen. Sarah took the servants' stairs up to the first floor and went into each bedroom where all the beds were covered with linen sheets. The house had been put to sleep over fifteen years ago but Sarah was determined to wake it up. She then went up to the servants' quarters on the top floor and had a look around up there. By the time Roderick had risen, she had explored the whole of the house and had made her mind up what she was going to do.

Roderick had come down and gone into the large kitchen where Sarah had made porridge for them both and black tea. They sat at the long pine table and discussed what they wanted to do and Roderick said, 'As far as I am concerned, you may run the house as you like and put your own stamp on it, if I am left alone to run the inn.' So that was how they proceeded, Sarah took over the house and the estate and Roderick ran the coaching inn.

As the weeks passed, Sarah transformed the house, she removed all the cobwebs, spring cleaned all the rooms and removed all the dust that had accumulated over the years. The house smelled of cleanliness: she was a Quaker lady and they believed in order, cleanliness and purity. At last, the house was beginning to awake.

Abel helped her with much of the work, but it was obvious that the years had taken a toll on him, and, like old horses, he walked very slowly. Sarah knew that the work was getting a little bit too much for him and she knew in her heart of hearts that she needed help with Cheswardine as it was a large house, too large for Sarah to manage on her own.

So one night she decided that she would discuss the situation with Roderick and see if he had any solution to the problem. Being a very shrewd woman, she decided to put the proposition to him in bed, which she thought, would give her a considerable advantage. Therefore, when Roderick came home from the inn one night and they went to bed, she said, 'I need to talk about Cheswardine with you' and he replied, 'Alright, tell me what you think.'

She said, 'There is a hiring fair in a week's time in the local town; I would like to hire a woman to help with the house.'

Roderick said, 'That's acceptable,' but Sarah continued, 'In the long term, I would like to farm Cheswardine because I think there is a lot of potential there.' At this Roderick sat up in bed and said, 'You want to farm Cheswardine? How?' and she said, 'I farmed with my father and my sisters, I understand farming. I have walked around the fields and the woodlands and I think there is great potential for Cheswardine. It has just been left and neglected over many, many years. The acreage is not as big as it used to be but there are roughly 200 acres of pastureland and 90 acres of oak, beech and elm and there is an income there if we harvest it right.' Roderick then realised that he had married not only an attractive and beautiful woman but also a highly intelligent one.

He said to her, 'How do you intend to make the farming pay?' to which she replied very simply, 'There is enough good pastureland to graze cattle and there are enough good arable fields to grow the corn. We can take some of the large oaks out of the woodland, which will provide us with an income as well because English oak is always in demand. Some of these trees are over 200 years old and they are worth quite a considerable amount of money.'

Roderick was a little taken aback as he realised that Sarah was going to be an extremely good businesswoman and farmer. He said to her, 'How do you intend to start?' to which she replied that initially she would like to buy two in-calf heifers to start the milking herd, from those she wanted to breed some good milking cows and from then on she would turn the milk into cheese. To increase self-sufficiency and for good farm practice, she intended to feed the whey to the pigs.

Roderick asked, 'If you are going to make cheese, what are you going to do with it when you have made it?'

She replied, 'We will send it to London and once we have pigs we will cure them and we will send them to London too. The cheeses, bacon and ham will all go to London as there is always a ready market in the taverns for good country produce.'

Roderick was taking this all in and frankly he was a bit stunned at everything that she had thought out but he could not see any disadvantage in the plan his wife had formed. Sarah said she would need twenty-five guineas to finance the start-up of the farming enterprise.

Roderick thought for a moment then said, 'We can manage twenty-five guineas if that will be enough,' to which Sarah replied, 'We will make it enough and we will be satisfied to start in a small way with what we have.'

It was agreed that Roderick would finance the new enterprise so Sarah decided that she would go to the local hiring market and fair where she would purchase the in-calf heifers, some piglets and various other animals and she would also engage a serving girl. Therefore, the next morning she said to Abel that, if he would get Jess ready on Wednesday morning, they were going to the hiring fair and the auction. He looked at her very strangely and asked, 'What for?'

She replied, 'We are going to awaken the farm, Abel, and we are going to put some life back into as it has slept too long.' Abel looked a little bit puzzled but he had lived long enough to realise that she knew which way she was going and he was willing to follow her on that path.

Come Wednesday morning, Abel got Jess out and put her in the shafts of the trap so they were ready to go to the market and the hiring fair. Sarah came out and got into the trap and Abel sat next to her. It took about an hour and a quarter to get to the market, and as they joined the winding roads the traffic grew heavier as it was quite an event in the farming year – not only was it an auction of cattle and sheep but also a hiring fair. The fair was held each year and any workers who wanted to be hired in agriculture or for large country houses all gathered and made a social occasion for all.

As they arrived at the fair, Abel said that they would leave Jess just outside the auction, and they would put a feedbag on him so he could munch while they were looking around the fair. Sarah said to Abel that first she wanted to look at who was available for hire. At the hiring fairs everyone advertised their trade by what they carried: cooks held a wooden spoon; shepherds had a crook; farm labourers carried a shovel; kitchen maids held a brush and grooms held a piece of rope. As they entered the fair,

Sarah walked down the narrow lane where the labourers were standing with all their different implements. Hiring maids would have a blue ribbon in their hair and cooks had a red ribbon so that you could distinguish what sort of duties they were skilled at.

As she walked down the lane, Sarah noticed a rather tall, skinny-looking girl and asked her, 'What are your skills?'

'I am a good cook, I can make good bread and soups and I worked for my sister in the kitchen attached to an Inn.'

She then said to another woman, 'What are your skills?'

The woman replied, 'Well, I worked in a busy coaching inn in north Staffordshire. It was on the main coaching road so we had to provide good food for weary travellers and that is what we did. We raised our own pigs, we kept our own chickens, we had our own cattle, and one of my duties was to cure the pigs.'

Sarah thought she had struck gold and thought this girl would suit her perfectly. If she had worked in an inn, she would be used to hard work as the doors of a coaching inn never closed. They were open twenty-four hours a day as the coaches came in morning, noon and night. Sarah knew she would be a hard worker. She said, 'Why have you come to this part of the world looking for a situation?'

The woman replied, 'I really wanted a change and to see if I could have a different type of life.'

Sarah asked her, 'What are you actually looking for?' and she said simply, 'Happiness,' which really struck Sarah, so she asked her name and she said, 'My name is Emma.'

Sarah asked if she could start immediately. She replied, 'Yes, I can,' so Sarah explained, 'We can pay you twelve guineas a year with everything found, aprons, hats and shoes provided,' and Emma said that that would suit.

With everything agreed, Emma and Sarah walked back to the cart where Emma put her belongings under the front seat. Sarah then said to her, 'I am now going to buy some livestock and, if you would like to come with me, we could get to know each other a little better.' It seemed that they had struck an immediate friendship, which rarely happens in this world of ours, they liked each other and they felt immediately comfortable with each other.

So Sarah, Emma and Abel proceeded to the cattle auction which was crowded with many different types of livestock. As the three walked between the pens, Sarah looked carefully at the various calves and in-calf heifers for sale. Abel pointed out to Miss Sarah an in-calf Ayrshire cow that he thought had a good structure and a good udder which he thought would be well worthwhile considering.

Sarah looked at him and said, 'No I really do not want that one, Abel, as I do not like the look of its face.'

Abel was completely stunned: he had never known anybody in his life buy cattle by the look on their face but, as a wise man, he decided to keep his comments to himself and followed behind.

Then Sarah stopped at a pen where there were two Jersey in-calf heifers, she looked at the faces of both of them and she decided that they were the ones she would buy. They were light brown in colour, one with a star on its forehead and the other with a white streak down the middle of its face and both were in good condition. She said, 'These are the cattle to start our milking herd because they are Jerseys, they will give good milk and cream, and that will make us a strong cheese.'

Emma agreed, 'Yes, they will be easily managed because they are a smaller type of cow and the milk that they give will be of excellent quality as Jerseys are known to give good milk.'

Therefore, they decided that when these cattle came up for auction they would bid on them. They continued walking through the market and saw all kinds of different animals but Abel decided that on this occasion, he would keep his opinions and advice to himself because he did not think it would be wanted.

Sarah said to Abel and Emma that next she would like to go to look at the pigs because she wanted to buy some piglets, so they headed for all the pens with the pigs. As was to be expected, there were many different types of pigs there, there were black and white spotted pigs, there were red pigs that were the Tamworths and there were black pigs, which were the Berkshires. Sarah walked down very deliberately until she came across a pen with ten black pigs in. She said to Emma that she thought these would be the ideal pigs to start the pig herd. Being a black pig, they could stay out when the sun shone and they would not have any trouble with them getting sunstroke, because with white pigs in the summer they would be forever having to get them to bathe to keep them cool. Sarah said that these would be stronger pigs and, when they were slaughtered, the black skins would be of use to the tanner and so they would have a good return on them.

Sarah reached into the pen and, putting one hand on its stomach and one in the middle of its back, she lifted one of the pigs out and felt that it had got a good stature, a good strong hind quarter and small shoulder and head. She said, 'These are the pigs we will bid for,' and, as she returned it to the pen, the pigs all squeezed together to keep themselves warm. So they had decided on the purchases they were going to make to stock the farm. From Sarah's point of view, it was the first decision in creating the business as she planned it and as she had told Roderick. As he thought, it proved to be the truth that she understood farming.

It was the custom at auctions that a bell would ring when they started to sell all the livestock off so people would gather around the first pen. As usual at auctions, the cattle were sold first, the sheep were sold second, pigs were sold third and after came the chickens and the rest. The bell rang and Sarah went to see what price the cattle would fetch. The auctioneer stood at the first pen, which were black and white cattle. He said these were good cattle that had come from a well-known farm in the area and were ready to graze on good pasture.

'Have I any bids at all?' he called and one bid half a guinea and another bid a guinea and, as there were no further bids, the auctioneer knocked them down to the second bidder.

In the next pen were the Ayrshire cattle and the auctioneer said that these cattle were all in calf, from a good home and would make profit wherever they went. They started at a guinea, the auctioneer asked for any more bids and somebody said a guinea and a half. There was a pause and another man who was leaning on the pens bid two guineas and they were knocked down at that price.

Then came the turn of the Jersey cattle, the auctioneer said that they were good specimens and came from a good home and hopefully would go to a good home, and would be well on the road to profit. He then asked if there were any bids and somebody in the crowd said half a guinea. A few moments passed and Sarah put her hand up and bid a guinea. The auctioneer was taken aback and asked, 'Are you bidding, madam?'

She replied, 'Yes, sir, I am bidding.'

The auctioneer took her bid at a guinea, the other bidder went to a guinea and a half, Sarah said, 'Two guineas.'

The auctioneer said to her, 'You do realise, madam, that these are in–calf heifers which are about to calve.'

Sarah replied, 'I do, sir, and they are about a month off calving,' at which everybody laughed. The auctioneer realised that she had as much knowledge as any of his customers there and decided to accept her bid at two guineas and the Jerseys were knocked down to Sarah. Sarah commented that they were a little bit more expensive than she had expected but you have to pay for quality.

Sarah, Abel and Emma then made their way down to the pig section and waited for the auctioneer who was making his way down to the pens. Eventually he came to where Sarah was standing with the small pigs and he looked at Sarah, smiled and thought, 'I will not make the same mistake twice.'

The auctioneer came up to the pigs and said, 'These are large black pigs from a good home and a well-known breeder who is very successful. I will put the ten pigs in as one lot so can I have any bids?' Somebody said half a crown and Sarah bid one crown. The auctioneer looked around and asked if there were any further bids for the ten pigs and, after a pause, he said, 'Sold to the lady.'

A few minutes later, a man spoke to Sarah and asked, 'Are you the lady who has bought my pigs?' and Sarah said, 'Yes.'

He said, 'I hope they go to a good home as they have been well bred and they will give you a good return. If you treat them right, they will be right with you.' He felt in his pocket and fetched out a penny and pressed it into Sarah's hand and said, 'This is luck money, I always do this when I sell pigs and I feel that it will bring you luck.' Sarah gripped the penny and thought the day had ended well.

Sarah said to Abel and Emma, 'I think I should go to the paying office and pay for the animals we have bought today and then we should make our way back to Cheswardine. It is a long drive and we have the two in-calf heifers and the pigs to get home. When we get them home, they will have to be bedded down and fed, as it has been a long day for them as well as us.'

So they made their way to the paying office and, as usual, there were three lines: the first line was to pay for the cows, the second was to pay for the sheep and the third line was to pay for the pigs and the chickens so Sarah queued to pay for the animals that she had purchased. As she, Emma and Abel entered the office, one man started to clap and then the rest joined in. It was so unusual for a lady to go farming in those days and most lookers-on thought she has great spirit to do it. Farming isn't an easy business to be in; you don't do it for the money, you do it for the love and the satisfaction you get out of it and all those that stood in there were in the same position so they welcomed a newcomer to their community and clapped as they came in.

As Sarah's turn came to pay for the cattle, the man asked which farm they were to be booked to and she said, 'Cheswardine.'

He then said, 'It's nice to have Cheswardine back on the books. I hope we see you again and I wish you good fortune with the purchases you have made today.'

That was the day done so Sarah asked Abel to go and fetch Jess so they could load the pigs and get the in-calf heifers too. Abel went and fetched Jess and walked him down through the market to the pen where the pigs were. They first put straw onto the back of the cart and lifted each pig in. Sarah said, 'Make sure the pigs are well covered with straw as it will be a cold night and it will be their first night without their mother so they may be a little bit cold.' Abel put plenty of straw in the cart and proceeded to go and collect the in-calf heifers.

Abel suggested to Sarah that perhaps it would be a good idea to employ a drover to bring the two cattle and the pigs back to Cheswardine but she said, 'No, we will not employ a drover, the drover will have one thing in mind in that he will want to get to Cheswardine as quickly as possible. The cattle are well in-calf and I want them to be in good condition when they arrive at Cheswardine, so we will walk them ourselves, we will take turns between the three of us.' Abel could take the first turn she said, then Emma and then she would take her turn. They got the two heifers, put a halter on each and proceeded to make their way back to Cheswardine.

Their little procession had begun to look like Noah's Ark with the cattle, the pigs and Jess pulling the cart as they made their way to Cheswardine.

It took a long time to get home, well over two hours and all the party were getting tired. As they pulled into the drive, they saw two gypsy caravans. The caravans stopped and the occupant of the first caravan walked along to Sarah, who was sitting on the cart, and said, 'Madam, are you the lady of the house at Cheswardine?'

'I am,' she replied.

He then asked, 'Can we camp at the top end of the woods here as we have done for many years?'

Sarah agreed, saying, 'Yes, you can but only take the fallen wood. You can poach the rabbits and the hares and you can keep the lay-away eggs but don't take those in the clutches. Don't hunt the deer in the park and when you have finished, dig a hole to bury your rubbish and leave the place as you found it.'

He looked rather stunned, but Sarah had lived in the country for a long time and she knew how things were done. She said, 'Furthermore, I would be obliged if you wouldn't borrow my stallion for any of your mares.' He looked puzzled but the practice was usually that when gypsies came to a new site where there was a stallion with a good bloodline, when their mares came into season, they would take them down in the middle of the night and have them serviced by a good stallion. However, she had lived in the country all her life, she had farmed with her father and knew how everything ticked.

Gradually they got up to the house and drew into the yard, and Sarah said to Abel, 'The first thing we must do is to bed down the heifers.'

Abel said, 'Shall we put them in the cow stalls?'

Sarah replied, 'No, we will put them into the looseboxes because if they calve early I don't want them chained as that will be a disadvantage.'

Therefore, she put them together in a large loosebox and then she said to Abel, 'Don't give them a drink straight away, we will let them settle down but if you get some clean straw we will wipe them all down and leave them for twenty minutes. Then give them a drink of water and feed them on some good corn and good hay and that should settle them for the night.'

Then she went for the pigs. Emma went with her and Sarah said, 'The first thing we will do, we will put the weaners in one of the looseboxes. We will get some straw and make a ring in one of the corners. Then we will fetch the pigs out one at a time and put them in the straw as it is the first night without their mother. I will go and fetch two stone hot water bottles and put them under the straw so that will cuddle them nice and warm through their first night.'

Abel went to Jess, took him out of the shafts, and settled him down for the night too.

Sarah said to Emma, 'It has been a long day for the animals and for us too and I think it is time we had some supper.' They went into the house and into the kitchen and Sarah said to Emma,

'I shall show you where everything is so you can cook some supper for us all, as I think we all deserve it for this day's work.'

Sarah left Emma in the kitchen, went into the study and the dining room, and closed the shutters as the nights were becoming cold and she wanted to retain the warmth in the house. She then went back to the kitchen where Emma had prepared a cold collation of cold meats, cheese, pickles and fresh bread. Sarah asked Emma if she had found everything she needed and Emma told her she was familiar with the running of a kitchen and had found everything. Sarah told her that after supper she would take her to her room, which would be on the second floor. Emma thanked her.

After supper, Sarah showed Emma to her room: she was very pleased and thought it was a lovely room. Sarah then said to her, 'I will see you in the morning and we will start a new age, a new experience, so, for now, I will wish you good night.'

Sarah went back to the kitchen and waited for Roderick, hoping he would not be too long. When Roderick arrived, having stabled his horse, he said, 'I have seen the two in-calf heifers and the pigs. Is this the start of the beginning?' at which they both laughed.

Sarah said, 'Yes, Roderick, do you want to know how much money I have spent?' but he looked at her and laughed, 'No, I know you Quaker ladies will spend money wisely and prudently, so the arrangement is you run Cheswardine and I will run the inn. I will stick to my side of the bargain and I am sure you will stick to yours.' With that, Sarah took Roderick's hand and squeezed it and she knew they were going to have many years of happiness.

Roderick and Sarah were up early the next morning as they knew it was going to be a big day for both of them, Roderick was expecting a lot of coaches at the inn that day so he wanted to set off early. Sarah wanted to look at the livestock she had and review the situation. Whilst she was sitting in the kitchen, Abel came to see her, saying, 'I have a surprise for you, Miss Sarah. One of the in-calf heifers has calved overnight and you have the nicest little heifer I have seen for a long time.' That started the day with a lot of happiness, so it was a good start.

Emma had been up early too and started tidying the kitchen, then she and Sarah had coffee together. Sarah said to her, 'Shall we go down to the stables and see the new arrival?' so they walked together down to the yard. A wonderful sight met them there, the heifer had calved just one calf; it had bright eyes, was a beautiful golden colour and had a white star on its head, just above its eyes. Sarah was delighted and thought she could have no better beginning than this. They then went to look at the piglets who were crying for their breakfast so Sarah and Emma fed them and the cows. Sarah encouraged the calf to suckle by putting some milk from the cow's teat on her finger and then putting her finger in the calf's mouth. It soon understood what to do and was happily feeding from its mother.

When Abel, Sarah and Emma had finished the outside work, Sarah told Emma that it would be a good idea if she showed her the house next as she would be running the outside areas and Emma would organise the household. They went back to the house and Sarah conducted a tour of the entire house and all the areas that would be Emma's responsibility. She showed her the two kitchens, the main one and the preparation kitchen, the laundry, the larder and she said, 'If you run the house the way you want to, there will be no interference from me as all I expect you to do is to keep the house clean and warm and provide nourishing meals. Abel will bring all the logs; there are only three of us in the house to be fed, Roderick, you and me. We will not be using most of the house so I do not think it will be too difficult to run.'

Sarah took Emma all over the house and showed her all the bedrooms and all the downstairs rooms so she could judge how much she needed to do. Sarah told her she would leave Emma to work out her own schedule for running the house.

Sarah had decided she would need more capital to start up the farming business at Cheswardine, so she decided to inspect the wood to see what saleable timber there was. She went and asked Abel to harness Jess, as she wanted to go round the woods to inspect the quality of the standing timber. Abel agreed and asked Sarah if she wanted him to accompany her, which she did. So Abel fetched some yellow string to identify the saleable timber, harnessed Jess and they both set off in the cart.

As they travelled through the woods, it was obvious the land had had little attention over the past hundred years. They saw elms, ash and mighty oaks and Sarah remarked, 'These will fetch good money if we can find a ready market for good timber, there is an abundance of good timber here.'

They worked their way through the woods and marked with yellow string each tree that was to be felled and sold. It took the best part of a day to go all through the woods as there was ninety acres of woodland but most of it was overgrown and had never been managed properly. Sarah's plan was to rid the woods of the old wood and make way for new trees. This was a good decision as it would help awaken Cheswardine and the money from the timber would help the restoration of the estate.

As they returned to the house, Sarah asked Abel to contact the woodman to start the felling and she would contact a timber buyer to negotiate a price. Abel agreed to contact the woodman to fell the trees but said they would need heavy horses or bullocks to pull the wood out of the forest and also to bring the hay in and later help with the harvest, as Jess and Mr Roderick's horse were not suitable for the task. Sarah agreed they would need heavy horses and realised it was a necessary investment. 'We will go tomorrow to the horse purveyor, the best one in the county is Willie Jack.'

Abel said, 'There is a horse fair in about a fortnight where we could probably buy some reasonable horses,' but Sarah disagreed, 'No, we want a good blood stock line, so we will go to the purveyor. We want to know the providence of the horses we have bought and, if we go to a man who breeds good horses and sells good horses, we will have value for money. If we go to a horse fair, there is a chance we could take a good horse home or we could buy a lot of trouble, so will buy them from a good horse dealer. We will go tomorrow to Willie Jack and purchase them.'

Sarah asked Abel to have Jess harnessed early in the morning so they could make their way to Willie Jack's as it would take them a couple of hours to travel there.

The next morning as arranged Jess was ready in harness and Abel and Sarah set off for Willie Jack's. It did take a couple of hours for them to reach their destination and as they were approaching the farm they could see it was well-kept. They went straight past the house and into the yard where a groom greeted them and asked them if he could be of service. Sarah replied that he could, she wanted a word with Willie Jack as she was in a position to purchase some horses so the groom said he would fetch him.

Within fifteen minutes Willie arrived; he was a large florid man, about six foot one, with a round face and a swagger in his step. He approached them, saying, 'Good morning, Madam, good morning, Sir. How can I be of service?'

Sarah replied, 'I am looking to buy two heavy horses for farm work.'

Willie told them he had several for sale and, if she cared to follow him, he would show her the horses. They went past the stables and in the field beyond there were two heavy horses. They were both Suffolk horses, very large horses of at least sixteen hands. Willie told Sarah they had some Suffolks and also some Clydesdales but for heavy work he thought the Suffolks were the best. Sarah asked how old they were and the dealer answered that one was four years old and the other was five, one was named Samson and the other Delilah. 'You will find they are good horses.'

Sarah asked the groom if he would run one of the horses around the field so she could watch him move. The groom did as he was bid and took Samson around the field; Sarah then asked for him to do the same with Delilah. Willie Jack watched Sarah and thought to himself, 'She's not a foolish lady at all.'

Sarah said, 'They are not wind broken and I like the stature of them and I also like the colour!'

Willie Jack said, 'You do not buy horses on the colour but on the breed,' and they both laughed. He said to her, 'I have shown you the best horses I have, Samson and Delilah. They are farm horses, a good breed and a good size and you will have many years of hard work out of them, as long as you treat them with goodness and kindness. Feed them well and shoe them frequently and you will have good service out of them. Talking about the colour of horses, I will take you to show you a mare, Bluebell. Now, she is a lovely colour and she is what we call in the trade a love horse, her mother was a Yorkshire coach horse and her father a hunter. He jumped the fence one day and the outcome was the foal Bluebell. She has grown into a good filly and she is a lovely horse. The reason I want to show you Bluebell is that she is one of the best-bred horses on the stud, but she is an unusual colour. So to prove my point, you do not buy the colour, you buy the horse,' and they both smiled.

Sarah was impressed with the quality of the horses he had shown them. Sarah told Willie Jack she liked the horses Samson and Delilah and she thought they would suit them well. The next stage in the procedure was to discuss price. Sarah also said she was taken with Bluebell and added, 'I will take your experience and advice, you do not ride the colour, you ride the horse. I think Bluebell will be an ideal mount for my husband as his horse is coming to the end of his useful life and is ready for retiring.' Sarah asked the price of the three horses.

Willie looked at her and said, 'I will take fifteen guineas for the three horses, and a total of twenty-one guineas for the harness and to shoe. I will shoe Samson and Delilah for the field, as they need different shoes for fieldwork and I will shoe Bluebell for the road.'

He was prepared to throw in the harnesses for the working horses for twenty-one guineas. Sarah looked at Willie Jack and knew he would not be prepared to negotiate, as it was a fair price. She agreed to the price and they both shook hands, as was the custom. Sarah then counted out twenty-one guineas into his hand, he took the money and then gave her one guinea back saying, 'This is your luck money,' as was the custom in those days, so the deal was done.

Willie Jack told her he would send the grooms over with the horses the following morning, they would be in full harness and there would be a pigskin saddle for Bluebell, good tack for good horses. Sarah thought she had made a good deal, they had bought some good horses for the money and everyone seemed to be happy with the outcome. Sarah and Abel made their way back to Cheswardine, all was right with the day they has just spent.

The horses arrived the following morning and Abel put them into loose boxes. Samson and Delilah were next to each other and Bluebell had her own loose box as well. Evening came and Roderick returned home knowing that Sarah had bought him a horse.

As he rode into the yard and dismounted, Sarah came out, kissed him and told him to come and look at his present. He walked into the stables and along the passageway; Bluebell popped her head out of her stable to greet them. Roderick was taken aback and said, 'She's a well-bred horse, good shoulders and will ride well but she is a most unusual colour.'

They both looked at each other and Sarah said, 'I have this from an expert, you ride the horse and not the colour!' They both laughed and Roderick gratefully accepted the gift from Sarah.

They went into the house and sat talking while eating their supper. Roderick said to Sarah that he intended to go to the cockfight the following day at Butters Hill. Sarah told him she did not agree with such cruel sports and she did not think that he should go. Roderick told her he would be going as it was a regular occurrence every year, he could catch up with his friends and acquaintances, and he could take Bluebell for a good ride. Sarah reiterated she did not agree with cockfighting and did not want him to go. They had both aired their views but Roderick instructed Abel to saddle up Bluebell for the next morning.

Roderick arose early the following day and told Sarah again that he was going to the cockfight. Sarah repeated that she did not approve and wished he would not go but Roderick he had made up his mind. Abel had saddled up Bluebell and she was waiting in the yard, so he mounted Bluebell and rode off to Butters Hill.

When he arrived, there was a large number of people milling about, there were stalls selling food and drink, toffee apples, stalls selling roast lamb, roast pork, and there were pie stalls. There were also a great many stalls selling porter and beer, it was a big annual event and most of the county were there.

The cockfight took place behind a wicker fence, the cocks were put into the arena and the spectators stood around the perimeter betting on their favourite cock. Roderick dismounted and took Bluebell to the stables where the stable hands took care of the horses; they told Roderick it would cost him a penny for his horse to be looked after. They took the saddle off Bluebell; Roderick gave the stable lad a penny and told him to look after Bluebell well and not to give her any water for a couple of hours or she would have stomach cramps. He told the boy he would be back in a couple of hours, knowing the ostlers would look after his horse.

Roderick made his way to the cockfight where there were gentlemen with top hats, gypsies in their bright coloured hats and many others; farmers, landed gentry, farm labourers, tradesmen of all description as it was a day out for all. The first cockfight began; the cocks were old English game, Cornish game and Indian game and there were many different breeds especially bred for fighting. Most people had bred their own cocks for fighting; it was a form of income for the farm labourers, foundry workers and the miners. It was their annual day out and there would be a great deal of money changing hands.

The procedure was that the cocks each wore a hood and a man would remove the hood from his animal and put the cock in the ring and then it was a fight to the death. It was a very vicious sport; the cocks would take one look at each other and attack. In most cases, the cocks fought to the death but, if one cock was too badly maimed, the owner would wring its neck to put it out of its misery. There was only ever one winner and it was a very cruel sport, but the men enjoyed it and it was always a welcome day out. There was a man who took bets and gave the odds and the betting was brisk.

Roderick decided he would stand and watch for a few rounds and then he would put a bet on one of the cocks. He was standing by the barrier as the next fight was arranged, more sawdust was put into the ring as the last fight had been a very bloody occasion. The next fight was the cock of a man called Crumpton Pierce, who was supposed to be the best breeder of fighting cocks in the county. The one he had bred was an all black cock from old English game stock and the other was an Indian game cock. Roderick went to the man who took the bets and told him he wanted to put a guinea on Crumpton Pierce's cock and the man said he would give him five to one; it had no chance against the Indian game. The cocks were brought to the ring and placed down; the old English game bird attacked the Indian game bird viciously and within a minute had killed his opponent.

Roderick went to collect his winnings and the man said, 'You chose well, here is five guineas plus your original stake.' Roderick decided as he was ahead of the game and had won five guineas he would go home. He went back to fetch Bluebell from the stabling yard and rode back to Cheswardine.

He arrived at Cheswardine and Abel greeted him in the yard, he told Abel to take Bluebell back to the stables and give her a good rub down as she had had a hard ride. Roderick then went into the house, down the hall and into the main kitchen.

Sarah greeted him with a smile but no kiss, as she was still cross with him for going to the cockfight. Roderick told her he had done well at the cockfight, he had made a profit of five guineas and he wanted her to have the money. 'You can buy yourself the best bonnet in town,' but Sarah replied, 'I do not want the five guineas. I do not want any reward from a wicked and cruel sport. You must keep the five guineas. I do not want a bonnet from the proceeds of such a cruel sport.' Roderick knew had made a mistake and underestimated Sarah, and knew he should not have gone to the cockfight.

When the time came for the evening meal, he looked at his plate, told Sarah it looked very nice and asked what was in the dish. She replied, 'It's chicken and it will be chicken for every meal including breakfast while you go to cock fights.' He looked surprised, 'Chicken for every meal, even breakfast?' 'Yes,' she replied, ' I have told Emma to serve chicken for every meal until you stop going to the cockfights and have assured me you will never go to another one.'

The next morning at breakfast, Roderick looked up as Emma came through the door bearing a dish, upon which was chicken. Roderick looked at the chicken and said to Sarah, 'I see you meant what you said.'

Sarah replied, 'Without a shadow of doubt, I told you breakfast, lunch and dinner until you promise me you will not go to the cockfight again.'

Roderick realised he had blotted his copybook and he capitulated and said, 'I made a mistake and I won't go to the cockfight again.' He was not a foolish man and realised the whole incident was the cause of the first row they had had.

Sarah replied, 'I accept your apology and consider the matter now closed. We will not discuss it again.'

Time went by at Cheswardine; the woodsman had taken the oaks out of the woodland, they had felled seven huge oaks, one of them being forty feet long and another fifty feet long. They were brought down to one of the fields near the house, and Sarah contacted the timber agent who purchased timber for the navy. As the country was still at war with Napoleon and the ships were built of oak, there was a great demand for English oak for ship-building.

The agent arrived on the appointed day at Cheswardine. He rang the bell and Emma answered the door. He told her he was John Grant and wished to speak to the person who was dealing with the sale of the timber as he had come to buy it. Emma went to fetch Miss Sarah and explained the situation. Sarah went through to the hall and shook hands with John Grant who said, 'It is most unusual in these times to deal with a woman in these matters,' and she replied, 'I hope that is not a barrier to us doing good business.'

He smiled, 'I hope not, Madam. I know what I want, you know what you want, and I am sure we can reach an agreement.'

They proceeded down to view the felled oaks, John Grant taking his measuring stick with him, which expanded to fully six foot, in order to measure the oaks. He inspected them carefully and stated, 'They are fine oaks, Madam, and they are English oaks not Welsh oaks, which are better as they have a finer grain. I think they are good timber and will be welcomed. Now, let us arrive at a price. I will make you one price for the timber, Miss Sarah, and I will remove them. I will have to bring up the bullocks and the carts as they are heavy timber and we will need a team of bullocks to remove them. We will bring a hoist and hoist them onto each cart, this will be the easiest way to move them. Now, let us get down to the price. I will give you twenty-five guineas for each tree, which is reasonable as we have our expenses once I have bought the timber. I have to transport it to the shipyards but the timber is good so I am offering you a good price.'

Sarah looked at him and accepted his offer of twenty-five guineas for each tree, then suggested they go back to the house to finalise details. They went back to Cheswardine and into the main kitchen; Sarah indicated for John Grant to sit down and told him she would arrange for some refreshments. John Grant took off his money belt before he sat down, as he did so a shower of golden guineas fell out. He counted out one hundred and seventy-five guineas into a line. Sarah then counted them and asked him if he wanted a receipt and he said he would be obliged if she did. Sarah wrote the receipt in beautiful copperplate writing, for the sale of seven English oaks from Cheswardine estate to Mr John Grant. She handed him the receipt and thought to herself, 'Cheswardine has been awakened and the renovation of the estate is beginning.'

Sarah poured him some tea and offered light refreshments, which was very welcome. He looked at Sarah, 'It was very pleasant conducting business with you and, if you wish to sell any more timber on another occasion, if you get in touch with me I shall be pleased to conduct business with you again.' He drank his tea, shook hands with Sarah and went on his way.

The weeks went by, the other heifer had calved, and with the other cow that had calved, there were now two cows producing milk. Once the calves were fed, the milk yield was six gallons a day in the summer and one gallon each day in the winter.

To start with, they fed the milk to the pigs but Sarah said to Emma, 'We could turn the milk into cheese or butter but the best way for Cheswardine is to make a special salted butter and put it in a small barrel or firkin and put it on the coach to London. We would have a good market as there is always a good sale for country butter and London is the best place.'

So Sarah contacted the ironmonger; the agriculture ironmonger being the man who sold everything to the farming community: rakes, barrels, scythes, kettles, sharpening tools, salt.

The ironmonger came to the house and Sarah went out to greet him. She explained that she wanted four sacks of Liverpool large grain salt and four barrels with lids as containers; the deal was completed to Sarah's satisfaction. She then told Abel she wanted him to open up the old dairy, whitewash the walls, and give the place a thorough clean. She told him to put plenty of salt in the whitewash to deter the flies from going on the walls; this was an old wives' way of doing things.

Abel started to work, he washed the walls, tarred the bottom, scrubbed the butter churns and cleaned the dairy until it sparkled and everything was ready to make Cheswardine's salted butter. When it was all ready, Sarah said to Emma, 'We will make the butter to start with and, if the butter trade gets busy, we will employ a dairy maid to make the butter on a regular basis.'

There was an abundance of milk so they decided to go ahead and make the first Cheswardine salted butter. The first thing they did was to wash out the barrels and put salt round the rim of the barrel as a preservative. The milk was put into the butter churns and the churning process began, this is a long and arduous task but eventually the butter separated out from the milk. The next job was to remove the solids, put it on the table and spread salt over it. The butter was mixed well with the salt and it was then ready to place in the barrels. Then the whey was removed into buckets, the butter was then replaced in the firkin, into which more salt had already been put and the butter was pressed well down to make sure there was no air remaining in the firkin. The lid was replaced with some salt on the lid and, finally, a small mallet was used to knock the lid into place to make sure it was well sealed. Then the barrel was sealed by using hot tar; a tar spoon was used to spread the tar round the rim on the top and bottom and all the seams on the barrel. This firmly sealed the barrel so that, in warm weather, the butter would not spill through the seams. The tar would keep the barrel airtight and keep the butter fresh. This was the very first barrel and it was now ready to go to London.

Miss Sarah informed Abel she wanted the butter to go on the eleven o'clock coach so that it would arrive in London the following morning. She also wrote a note to the butter purveyor who supplied butter and cheese to the landed gentry. He wanted suppliers to sell him good quality food and Sarah was going to provide him with this.

A week went by and a letter arrived from the purveyor, which stated that the butter had arrived and it was in excellent condition. It had had a good reception from all his customers and the barrel had sold. He stated if the quality remained the same, he was in the market for four barrels of butter a week.

Sarah knew if she had to produce four barrels a week for the London market she would need help in the dairy so she asked Abel if he knew of anyone who had experience in the dairy and who would be interested in the position. Abel replied that there was a farm at the bottom of the valley that made butter and cheese and he was sure someone there would be interested. He would get in touch with them and see if the young lady might help.

When Abel contacted the lady who lived on the farm, she told him she was indeed very interested and would come for an interview when it was convenient. Miss Sarah sent a message with Abel to say that any morning would be convenient as long as she notified her which day. The reply stated that she would come next Thursday morning.

Sarah made sure she was ready, the young lady arrived promptly at eight-thirty in the morning. When Sarah greeted her and asked her name, the young lady replied, 'My name is Sian, and I live with my mother and father on the small farm at the bottom of the valley.'

Sarah said, 'Let's talk about the position in the dairy. Do you have any experience of butter and cheese making?'

'Yes, I have, we make all our own butter and cheese and sell it in the local markets,' replied Sian. 'We have never had any difficulty selling our butter and cheese as we make a good quality product. I learned how to make butter and cheese when I was a child and have always helped in the dairy with my mother and father, so I do understand the process. I would work hard for you and produce a good product for you if you are willing to give me a chance.'

Miss Sarah explained to Sian that the position was to make good quality butter for the London market and she would be required to live in. The salary would be fourteen pounds a year and her uniform of a dairy maid's pinafore and hat would be provided. Sarah told her the duties would involve keeping the dairy clean, including keeping all the shelves clean and tidy. The floor would need to be scrubbed and, in the summer, the shutters would have to be closed to keep the sunlight out, and these too would need cleaning.

All the utensils must be scalded to keep them clean as this is the secret to a successful dairy. Her duties would involve milking the cows early, the udders thoroughly cleaned before milking, and the udders emptied properly as, if not, the milk yield would decrease. Whilst they were being milked, the cattle must be given their fodder and carrots. Sarah explained that it was essential that Sian should milk the cows each day as they get used to the same person milking them. If a cow has sore teats, it is advisable to wash the teats in warm water twice daily and apply a balm if necessary.

She explained that a cow should give you roughly three gallons a day and a gallon in the winter and that should produce about one and a half pounds of butter a day. If there is any surplus whey or milk left over once the house has had their milk for the day, the surplus should be given to the pigs. Pigs thrive well on milk and whey and then good bacon is produced from the meat.

Sarah said, 'The position is yours and, if you accept, you can start next Monday.'

Sian replied, 'Thank you very much. I would like to accept the position and I will be here early next Monday morning.'

Miss Sarah said, 'I hope you will be very happy here. I will go and fetch Emma so she can show you your bedroom and show you around so you are familiar with the house and dairy.'

Sarah was pleased with the girl as she looked clean and she knew the business of the dairy well and this seemed to be another step in turning Cheswardine into a prosperous concern.

Sarah knew the London market was going to expand so she thought she should get in touch with the agricultural ironmonger who supplied all the barrels for the butter. He supplied three types of barrel; the hogshead, which was a large barrel; a middle-sized barrel and the firkin. The firkin was ideal for the butter as it was small and easy to handle. Sarah knew she would also have to order some Liverpool salt; she wanted two types of salt, the large grain and the small grain. The large grain was to put in the whitewash to paint the stables, the dairies and the styes; this was put into the lime to keep the mixture firm and to deter flies. She also wanted to add tar for the bottom of the dairy and the stables, this was painted around the lower part of the wall to stop the whitewash being swilled away when these areas were cleaned out. She sent a message to the agricultural ironmonger and he arrived the next day. Sarah ordered fifteen firkin barrels, six bags of lime, half a barrel of tar, six bags each of fine and large grain Liverpool salt; these supplies would now last her quite a while.

Time passed and the harvest was nearly ready to be brought in. Sarah knew that successful farming depended on luck and skill, but mainly on luck. She decided she would fetch the harvest in early this year as it was ready, then she would know how they stood for the winter.

She told Abel she would need the men from the village who helped with the harvesting to come to Cheswardine. She would need them for approximately six weeks to harvest the hay, corn and barley. Abel said he thought there would be about fifteen men available to help with the harvest and he thought she was right to harvest now before the weather broke. He went off to the village and recruited fifteen men, as was the custom. These men went from farm to farm helping with the harvest as there were few mechanical aids.

This was a big occasion on most farms and estates; the farmer was obliged to provide the men's food for the day, breakfast, dinner and tea. The men started at six o'clock in the morning and worked until the light went. It was a long day for the harvesters and it was a long day for the farmers' wives who provided all the refreshments. The refreshments usually consisted of bread and cheese, cold tea, farmhouse cake and a slice or two of cold ham. The labourers needed good sustenance as it was long, hard work.

The harvest was duly brought in, the straw was ready for the animal bedding and the corn had gone to be milled, ready for the winter feeding. Sarah looked back on her first year and thought how successful it had been, the estate had been revitalised and they were producing a good amount of butter for the London market. The Cheswardine estate was looking healthy, there had been a lot of skill, attention and love put into it and that was now being repaid.

CHAPTER 4

A Harvest Ball

Sarah thought that, as they had worked hard for nearly twelve months to make the estate a going concern, now was the time to have a ball, invite all the neighbours, and meet everyone formally. It was normal procedure to have some kind of festivity at this time of the year in the country. Sarah decided she would talk to Roderick on his return from the inn to see if he was in favour of having a ball. He was rather late that night but she waited in the kitchen for him to return and eventually she heard him in the yard. He came in the front door as was customary and then through into the kitchen. He asked if she had had a good day.

She replied, 'Yes, we have had had a good day. The last of the harvest was all brought in. Have you had a good day?'

He said, 'It has been a very busy day as there have been lots of coaches coming in today, it looks as if everything is beginning to pick up.'

Sarah told him she had achieved everything she had set out to do in her first year and then she told him of her idea of having a ball and inviting all the neighbours. Roderick replied, 'That's a very good idea and I think we will enjoy that.'

Sarah said, 'There is one proviso: I would like a fiddler, a flute player and a drummer but I do not want any alcohol as I do not believe in the drinking of alcohol.'

Roderick was lost for words, but when he recovered, he told her a ball without alcohol was like having a feast without bread. But Sarah was adamant and insisted that is how she wanted it to be. Roderick looked at her and eventually thought she was probably right – 'when drink's in, wit's out.' So he agreed with her and told her to organise the event. He asked her the date she was thinking of and she told him the beginning of October. Roderick thought that was a good time to have a ball as the farming calendar was coming to an end and the harvest was in.

Roderick said, 'This time of year is a bit dull and it would make Cheswardine come alive. We could meet all the neighbours as there has not been the time in the summer to socialise.'

The arrangements were made to have the ball at the start of October and Sarah asked Abel if he would deliver the invitations, as Sarah did not know many people. She asked Abel to tell her all the nearest farms, their names and who they should they invite. Abel went through the list and he asked her about a particular gentleman called Timothy Witt who farmed at High Hill. Abel told her he had a bad reputation for drinking and womanising and asked if she wanted to invite him.

Sarah said, 'We do not want to go on gossip so we will invite him out of courtesy and hope he enjoys the evening the same as everybody else.'

Abel said, 'Miss Sarah I think you are making a mistake but as you are the lady of the house I will abide by your instructions.'

Sarah told him she would get on soon with writing the invitations if he could find a member of staff to deliver them, as it would give the neighbours time to decide if they were free to accept or not. The list was completed and the invitations sent out.

Sarah talked with Emma regarding the refreshments for the ball and they decided they would have tea and coffee to drink. The food would consist of roast lamb and pork, also pork pies, and for dessert, a freshly-baked plum pie and that would be sufficient. There would be about thirty people coming and, once October came, a pig would be ready for slaughtering so there would be ample pork for the occasion.

Emma said, 'Where will you hold the ball?' and Sarah replied, 'We will hold the ball in the big hall where the fiddler, the flute player and the drummer will play. We will open the dining room where all the food will be set out.' So they continued with making all the arrangements.

Time went on and, when September came, Sarah said to Abel she thought some of the pigs were ready for slaughter and to be made into bacon. The pigs had been well fed on the whey from the butter making and they had also been given plenty of bran and household scraps so they were bonny looking pigs. She asked Abel to get in touch with the journeyman Master Curer; he came round all the farms and estates to process the pigs ready for curing and salting for the winter.

Abel said, 'Cedric Winters is the best curer and he has practised his profession for a long time and also the art of drinking but he does both jobs very well.'

Sarah smiled and told Abel to arrange for him to come in a fortnight's time, they would starve the pigs overnight so that they would be ready for Cedric to slaughter the following morning. The majority of the meat could be cured into bacon and hams for the winter.

The day came for the Master Curer to arrive and Sarah had made sure that the pigs had been starved overnight and that there was plenty of hot water in the dairy ready and waiting for him. Cedric arrived at seven o'clock in the morning, as an early start was wanted. He slaughtered the pigs throughout the day and processed them; he said he would return the following day to prepare them and asked Sarah what she wanted for fresh meat and what she wanted to salt down.

The next day Sarah met him in the dairy and asked him what he thought of the pigs and he told her he thought they were bonny pigs, light-fleshed and they would cure well. Cedric asked her which she wanted for bacon and which she wanted for ham and fresh pork. Sarah replied she wanted two of the legs for the coming ball and he could make the rest into bacon and hams. When he asked her if she had sufficient salt, Sarah told him she had Liverpool salt, both large and small. Cedric laughed and observed, 'You have done this job before,' at which she smiled and said that yes she had.

Cedric told her he had come from a farm down the road, Renshaws, and the pigs did not look as healthy as hers, and he was disappointed doing the job.

Sarah replied, 'Excuse me, but I do not want to hear any one else's business, only my own and I prefer not to deal in gossip.'

That took Cedric aback but he answered, 'Very well, Madam, as you will.'

Sarah said, 'I plough my own fields with my own horses and I do not have to touch my cap to anybody.' They both knew where they stood and Cedric knew he must not gossip about the neighbours, but should just do his job and put the pigs to ham and bacon.

Cedric began salting the sides and told the dairymaid he wanted the sides turned every day for a fortnight and to replenish the salt that had disappeared and turned into brine. Cedric told her that, after a fortnight, she should fetch the sides out and wash them off with clean tepid water, dry them and then hang them up in the dairy. He told Sian he had already put the string up in the right place ready for her to hang them up and he told her they were to hang in the dairy for a fortnight to dry out. Then she was to put pepper on the sides and wrap them in a linen cloth. They would mature well and there would be enough bacon to see them over the winter. When the job was completed, the bacon hung in lines and Cedric thought he had never seen a prettier sight; it was like dining with God.

Cedric asked Abel if he could see Miss Sarah as his job was completed. Abel took Cedric to Miss Sarah's office where she duly paid him for his labours and told him to take a flitch of bacon, as it had been a job well done. She shook hands with him and wished him well and he went on his way.

Invitations to the ball had been delivered and, as all had been accepted, Sarah knew the number of people coming would be about fifty. Sarah and Emma now had a good idea as to how much food would be needed. The arrangements all now started to fall into place, the food was planned, the dining room and the house had had a thorough clean. Logs were placed in the dining room ready for the fire and the musicians were engaged. There was still a fortnight to go but Sarah felt happier with all the arrangements in place.

Sarah told Abel she did not want the guests' horses standing in the cold, she wanted them out of harness and put in the stables. Abel thought she was very wise to organise this, if it was a bad night the horses would be standing in the cold for hours. Abel was to organise the coaches, their drivers would sit in the room in the stables where light refreshments would be provided for them. These arrangements were made, the horses and their drivers were catered for and the plans for the ball were well under way.

Sarah decided she would wait up for Roderick to come home that night to discuss with him all the arrangements for the ball. Roderick was late again that night; she heard the hooves of the horse as Bluebell galloped into the yard. He came into the kitchen and, smiling, said to Sarah, 'Luck has gone your way today.' When Sarah asked him why, he said he had bought a bolt of cloth from one of the travellers on the coaches and he thought she might like it to make a ball gown.

Sarah asked to see the cloth and she gasped with surprise as the material was so beautiful, it was blue with gold threads. The weaver who had made it was evidently a very skilled man and Roderick told Sarah he could not let the material go, as he knew she would look beautiful in a ball gown made from it. He asked her if there would be sufficient time to make the gown and Sarah told him she would make the time. Sarah gave Roderick a kiss and thanked him for the present; he replied, 'That is all you need to say.'

There was great happiness in the house; the estate was beginning to prosper and Roderick and Sarah were looking forward to hosting their first ball in the house in a fortnight's time.

The next fortnight produced a flurry of activity in the house; all the lamps had to be trimmed so they did not smell. The candles also needed replenishing, the carpets were taken up and the oak boards underneath polished for the dance floor. All the silver was cleaned and ready for use, the tables all polished and put into place. Everything was on course for the ball; a fire lit in the hall to take the chill off the house. The braziers, some at the front of the house and some in the stable yard, were ready to light up the house and stables, as the coachmen would need to be kept warm, too.

The remaining days passed quickly and the day arrived for the ball. Emma and the kitchen staff had been working hard for days to prepare all the food and now it was six o'clock in the evening. The musicians arrived and were in the kitchen, Sarah told them they would be playing in the hall. She took them through to the hall and told them she wanted them to stand either side of the fireplace. They asked her how long she wanted them to play to which she replied, 'As long as people want to listen!' They laughed at this and told her the lady had a lovely sense of humour.

The musicians positioned themselves where Sarah had told them and began to play, nobody had yet arrived as it was still early but the music seemed to bring the house alive. Sarah told Emma she was going upstairs to dress and make herself ready for her guests. Roderick was already in his dressing room making ready as he had arrived home early for this special occasion. As Sarah went upstairs, Roderick asked to see her new dress but Sarah told him he would have to wait until she was dressed. He replied, 'I will just have to sit here and wait for you, then,' and she replied smiling, 'Yes, you will.'

Sarah dressed herself in the new dress that she had made, she was a good seamstress and was pleased with the result. She dressed her hair with clips and a feather and, when she decided she was presentable, she called Roderick into the bedroom. Roderick could not believe the transformation and told her she was very beautiful, he was very proud of her and she would turn everyone's head that night. Sarah was happy, she had made a beautiful dress and she had pleased Roderick. She said to Roderick that they should be downstairs as the first guests would be arriving at seven o'clock so he gave her his arm and they went to greet their guests.

Sarah looked out of the window and saw Abel and Lyndon were filling the braziers with logs; it was a scene of happy anticipation. As the guests started to arrive, Sarah and

Roderick were there to greet them all and direct them into the ballroom where they were offered refreshments. The evening was progressing happily and all the guests seemed to be enjoying themselves, old friends meeting one another and discussing local affairs.

After some time, one gentleman approached Sarah and introduced himself as Timothy Witt and said he had not had the pleasure of being introduced when they had first arrived in the county. He wished them good fortune on the farm but he did have a complaint, that there was not any alcohol at the evening's event and he had never been to a ball where there was not any alcohol. Sarah looked at him and said, 'This is a Quaker household and we do not agree with alcohol.'

He replied, 'Yes, I was aware of that so I have brought my own supplies.'

Sarah said, 'I think that is very discourteous as we do not allow alcohol in the house,' but Timothy replied, 'That is your opinion and if I wish to bring my own supply of alcohol I will do so.'

Sarah drew herself up to her full height, 'Mr Witt, rudeness is given to us all but only used by the foolish.'

He answered, 'That's as maybe but you have not been long enough in farming to give me advice on my drinking habits or any other subject. You are a newcomer to farming and would do well to remember there is a lot of stumbling before you arrive at the top of the hill.'

Sarah looked at him and said, 'I think you are very discourteous and I believe it is time your coachman was called and you returned home.'

He looked startled, 'You wish me to leave?'

'Yes,' she replied, 'I wish you to leave. I think you are a very discourteous person and you are trying to spoil the evening and I think you have had too much alcohol.'

At this point, Roderick appeared, noticed the tension between them, and asked if there was a problem. Sarah replied, 'No, there is no problem. It has all been resolved. Mr Witt is saying goodnight and we wish him a safe journey home.'

Timothy Witt turned on his heel and marched out of the hall, picking up his cloak and slamming the door behind him.

The night was drawing to an end and some of the guests were beginning to leave and saying their farewells to Roderick and Sarah. All of them told Sarah and Roderick how nice it had been to meet them both and what a lovely evening they had had. The atmosphere in the old hall had been lovely and they were glad the house was being lived in and loved once again. Sarah agreed with them, the hall had been left too long and she was glad they had awakened the house.

As the last guests left, Sarah asked Roderick if he would like to go into the kitchen and have a nightcap, as she wanted to discuss something with him. Roderick agreed, he shut and locked all the doors, closed the shutters and then went into the kitchen where Sarah was waiting for him.

She asked him to sit down as she had something to tell him, which was important. Roderick sat down and waited for Sarah to begin speaking. She said, 'I think I am with child.'

He said, 'Are you sure?' and Sarah replied, 'Yes, I am. It is some months away yet but it will be the first child born at Cheswardine for a long time.'

Roderick was very pleased and hugged Sarah to him; he could not believe what a lucky man he was to have found Sarah. He told her he would organise the nursery and the nursemaid but Sarah told him it was her job to arrange all those matters and his role was to hold the baby at the christening. Roderick laughed and thought what a wonderful wife he had and that he was the luckiest man alive. As they climbed the stairs, holding each other's hand, they realised how much life had changed for both of them as they were going to bring a child into the world. They both knew the arrival of this child would brighten their future and make the bond between them even stronger.

CHAPTER 5

Family News

Sarah developed the bloom of pregnancy, as all women do; she wanted to share her happiness with Emma so she told her the child would be born in the next few months. Emma was very happy for her and said having a baby in the house would bring great joy.

Sarah sent for Abel and told him she wanted Jess harnessed in the morning so she could go and see her mother and father in the village. Abel said, 'So you will want to visit your parents to tell them the good news about the child.' Sarah was taken aback but Abel explained there are no secrets in the country, everyone knows each other's business and usually has an answer for everything and a solution to nothing! Sarah laughed and thought that was very funny.

The next day Abel put Jess into harness and Sarah set off for her parents' house. The autumn was fading and winter starting to take hold; the trees were losing their leaves but those that still remained were a beautiful golden colour. It was a very wooded part of the country and Sarah admired the scenery and the trees and looked forward to seeing her mother and father. Jess trotted along and seemed to be enjoying the outing as much as Sarah was. She thought how captivating moments like this were and how she would always remember this drive. Sarah enjoyed her own company and was happy just to enjoy the journey as they drove through the lanes.

They eventually arrived at her parents' house and, as she turned into the drive, she saw her father tending the flowers in the garden. He loved his garden and his flowers and there was still an abundance of late autumn colour. The cottage stood back from the road and the tranquillity of the scene was not lost on Sarah.

As Jess stopped outside the front door, Sarah alighted from the trap and went over to her father. They hugged each other and he told her it was lovely to see her and how pleased her mother and her sisters would be. Sarah told him she had news that she thought would make them happy so her father said they should go into the house so her mother could hear the news, too.

They went into the cottage where Sarah hugged her mother; then her father asked what news she brought. Sarah looked at them both and said, 'I think I am with child.'

Her father replied, 'We are all very happy for you. This will cement your marriage and make it even more loving and happy when there is a child in the house.' Sarah's mother hugged her too and told her she was very happy for her.

Her father told her he would take Jess out of the shafts of the trap and put him in the paddock, as he would enjoy the grass and a bit of freedom. Sarah thanked her father, as it would be a long time for Jess to stand waiting in the shafts.

The Quakers were good farmers with cattle and sheep; they looked after the land very well, which was a gift Sarah had inherited from her father and mother. The success Sarah had had at Cheswardine was due to all the skills she had learnt from them. Her father was a moderate man who did not shout his success from the rooftops but carried on with life no matter the trials and tribulations he encountered. He had passed this on to his family and, if happiness could be bought and sold, he would have a lot of happiness to sell.

Sarah's mother asked her if she wanted a light lunch as it was well past midday. Her sisters then came in from the dairy and shared in the joyous news. As was the custom in Quaker houses, the chairs were hung on pegs on the wall in the kitchen, which was a long room with a big oak table in the middle. At one end, there was the stove and a fire where all the cooking was done; Quaker women could produce nourishing, tasty meals from very simple ingredients, as their lifestyle was one of simplicity.

Sarah's father told them to sit at the table and a prayer was said before the meal. Throughout the meal, the talk was naturally about the baby and Sarah's mother said they would gather all their sewing threads and needles and materials and start making clothes for the baby so he will come into the world and be well-clad and everyone laughed.

Her mother told Sarah she still had the christening gown worn by her sisters and herself and, when the time was right, she would bring it over to Cheswardine for the new baby to wear for the christening. Then she went upstairs and fetched it; whoever had made the gown had put a lot of skill and love into the making of it. The gown had been well looked after and was in pristine condition. Sarah held it up against herself and said, 'Well, it would not fit me now,' and everyone laughed.

Her father told her that upstairs in the attic was their original crib, which had inscribed on it Sarah's name and her two sisters, and she was very welcome to use it when the time came and they would bring it over for her. Sarah thought that was a lovely idea; it was a link with her childhood and a link with her father who had made the crib and with her sisters as their names were on it as well. This crib represented a bond between the families and Sarah liked the idea that her baby would share the family link.

The occasion was a very happy one, the women talked and

laughed, the day went very quickly and it was soon time for Sarah to journey home. She went out into the garden where her father was tending the last of the autumn flowers. She greeted him and they talked about the garden and how much produce had been gathered. Then she walked round the house, remembered her childhood and all the happy times, and thought to herself how good life was and she hoped it would continue.

Sarah needed to be on her way before the evening started drawing in as it was a long drive to Cheswardine so her father put Jess in his harness and lit the lamps on the trap in case the light went before she arrived home. Sarah said her farewells to her sisters, hugged her mother and told her she hoped to see her soon; her mother told her to take care of herself and the baby. Her father put his arms round her and also told her to take care of herself and that they would see her later in the year, then he kissed her tenderly and helped her into the trap. Jess seemed impatient to go so Sarah waved goodbye to her family and he trotted off quickly down the drive.

As they travelled along, the light was beginning to fade when Sarah spotted a figure in the distance. It looked like a young girl and she seemed to be carrying a bundle of clothes. Then, as Sarah drew closer, she realised the girl had no shoes on. She drew level, pulled on the reins and Jess slowed and stopped. Sarah said, 'You are out late on these country roads, where is your destination?'

The girl replied, 'I am going to the other side of Hinckley as I have heard there is a position on one of the farms and I am making my way there in the hope of employment.'

Sarah asked her where had she come from and the girl answered, 'I used to work on a farm at the other side of Hinckley but unfortunately the owners died and the new owners brought their own staff with them so they did not want any of the farm's servants.'

Sarah said she had come a long way, to which the girl replied that she had been on the road for two days. When Sarah asked where she slept at night, the girl told her she slept under the hedges. Sarah then asked if she would like a lift as far as her own destination and the girl said, 'I would be very grateful, madam, for a lift.'

Sarah had one last question for her, 'Tell me, why do you not wear your shoes when they are round your neck?'

The girl replied, 'They are the only shoes I have and, if I wear them too much, I will wear them out then I will have none.'

Sarah told her to climb onto the trap and they would make haste as the night was drawing in and she did not want to travel in the dark. Jess seemed to sense the urgency and he trotted off at a brisk pace. They travelled along the winding roads and, after about an hour, they saw the lights of Cheswardine. Sarah asked the girl what she was going to do now and the girl replied she would sleep under the hedge for the night and then carry on in the morning to the farm.

Sarah said, 'No, you won't. You will come home with me and stay the night at Cheswardine; it is not right for a young girl to sleep out under hedges as the sky is full of rain and it will be cold.' The girl had no choice but to go with Sarah and to accept her kindness.

Sarah turned Jess in to the drive and, as they approached, they saw smoke coming from the chimneys and the lights shining out. Abel came to the door and said he would see to Jess and the trap, and for Sarah to go into the warm. Abel then noticed the girl and asked Sarah, 'Who is the lassie you have brought with you?'

Sarah replied, 'She is a gift and we never turn a gift away.'

Sarah then said, 'By the way, young lady, what is your name?' and the girl replied, 'Polly.' Sarah welcomed her to Cheswardine and said, 'Polly, come with me and I will prepare you some supper.' Abel took Jess away, took him out of the trap and his harness, rubbed him down with straw, fed and watered him and then stabled him for the night.

Meanwhile, Polly followed Miss Sarah into the kitchen. Sarah told the girl to warm herself against the fire and said she would ask Emma to give her some supper. Emma came into the kitchen, greeted Sarah and asked if she had had a nice day. Sarah replied that she had had a lovely day and the day had been nicer because she found Polly on the road. She had brought her to Cheswardine and, if she wanted to stop and work there, she would be very welcome as things would change now that she was with child and Emma would need extra help.

Sarah turned to Polly and said to her that there was a position at Cheswardine if she wished to stay. After looking thoughtfully at Polly, Emma said she thought that would be a good idea. Sarah asked Polly how long she had been at the farm and Polly replied, 'I was taken out of the orphanage when I was nine and I worked on the farm until now and I am fourteen years old, so I have always worked in the house and on the farm.'

Sarah said, 'You will be used to hard work, I am sure, so I will give you a chance to stay here at Cheswardine if that is what you would like.'

Polly was taken aback and said to Sarah, 'I would be very grateful of the chance, Mistress, and I will be sure to work hard for you.'

Emma soon prepared some supper and they all sat round the kitchen table; Polly ate as if she had not eaten for a while, much to the amusement of Sarah and Emma. Sarah told Emma to put Polly in one of the servants' bedrooms at the top of the house and she would instruct her in her duties in the morning.

When they had gone, Sarah sat quietly and thought through the day and what a lovely day it had been with her parents and her sisters, and then to meet Polly on the road was a piece of good fortune. Sarah had a feeling that Polly would be an asset to Cheswardine.

Sarah arose early next morning; Roderick had already left for the inn and Sarah wanted an early start to the day. When she arrived in the kitchen Polly was already there; Sarah said to her she had brought her another pair of shoes which she hoped would fit.

She had also brought some clothes down for her. Sarah told her she had started a new position and she had new clothes and new shoes for a new life; and now she had two pairs of shoes so she would not wear them both out together. Polly was so taken aback she did not know what to say. Miss Sarah told her she would pay her quarterly so she could buy herself some personal things from the local village.

Then Sarah wanted to speak with Emma to discuss the household duties as, now she was with child, she wanted the house to run as smooth as clockwork. Emma and Sarah sat round the kitchen table to discuss the running of the house and Polly's duties. Sarah thought it was a good idea to send a message to the midwife, Mrs Grace, to book her for when the baby was born. Emma thought it was rather soon but Sarah wanted to book her early to make sure she had her knowledge and expertise as it was her first baby and she did not want anything to go wrong.

So Sarah sent Abel down to the village with a message for Mrs Grace to come to Cheswardine to discuss the arrangements.

Polly's duties were discussed also and Emma thought the girl would be a great help in the kitchen and the dairy.

In due course Mrs Grace appeared at Cheswardine and asked to see Sarah; she was shown into library where Sarah was working. Mrs Grace was a tall, thin woman with her hair scraped back from her face; Sarah welcomed her and offered her a seat. They discussed details of the pregnancy and Mrs Grace gave Sarah some advice. She told her to remain as active as possible, eat plenty of good, nourishing food and take lots of rest in the later period as she would begin to feel tired.

Mrs Grace told her at the confinement she would need clean sheets, hot water and a crib for the baby. Sarah said the crib was already arranged and would be there when needed. Sarah then asked her what her fee would be, she told Sarah she would discuss that with her later when the baby was happy in this world and she was happy too. Sarah was naturally concerned, as it was her first baby, but she felt very confident in Mrs Grace as she had delivered so many babies.

By the time she left, Sarah felt a lot happier. After Emma had shown Mrs Grace out, she returned to the library, where Sarah repeated what she had been told: that clean sheets, hot water and the crib must be available and that Mrs Grace would stay until the baby had settled in. These arrangements made, life went on at Cheswardine.

Sarah decided to wait up for Roderick as he came in from the inn; she heard the horse's hooves on the cobbles as Roderick arrived back. She waited in the kitchen for him, he came in and put his arms round her, gave her a hug and a kiss and asked if she was all right. Sarah told him the midwife had been to see her about the birth. Roderick said to her, 'Good, but I think we should also have Dr Curtis to see you.' Sarah said she did not want the doctor as she felt very confident with the midwife who had delivered many babies in this area and she felt she wanted her to be there. Roderick replied, 'If that is what you want, I am happy for you to have the midwife.'

Sarah said, 'Polly, the new girl, is settling in well so I will be able to rest more as a lot of the workload has been lifted from my shoulders. As I now have some time, I would be interested to see the coaching inn and how it works, as I have never been there before. May I come with you tomorrow if it is convenient?'

Roderick looked at her in amazement, 'If that is what you want, you will be very welcome. We will go in the morning in the trap and take Jess with us.'

The next morning Jess was harnessed to the trap, Abel brought him round to the front door, they both got in and set off to the coaching inn. The road was winding until they reached the main coaching road but, once they reached the main road, they could see the inn in the distance. They arrived at the inn and drew into the coaching yard, which was very busy with coaches arriving frequently. One of the ostlers told them he would see to the pony.

Roderick explained how things worked at the inn: that the coaches arrived every hour; the horses had to be changed; the ostlers who looked after the horses walked them round to cool them down as they would develop a cold or chill if they were put straight in the stables. Roderick said that, when the coaches were half a mile away, the coachman would blow his horn so the ostler would know to get the horses ready for when the coach arrived.

On the coach's arrival, the horses would be taken one at a time out of harness, walked round the yard to cool down, and then put in the stables. The fresh horses, already harnessed, would then be attached to the coach. While this was happening, the passengers would alight and partake of refreshments in the inn. The passengers inside the coach would go into the parlour and outside passengers went into the vaults. Sarah asked why and Roderick told her the passengers who sit in the coach pay more for their fares than those who sat on the top of the coach so were entitled to a better class of service.

Roderick told Sarah to go into the parlour so she could see the type of food the passengers would be offered. Sarah went into the parlour and saw the array of food on the table. There were pickles, roast ham, beef, pork pies, pickled eggs, freshly baked bread and cheeses.

Sarah thought the display and variety was excellent and Roderick explained, 'Yes, we have to have a good menu for the coach trade as there is a lot of competition and if we provide good food the word is spread that this inn is a good place to stop. We do not make a lot of money changing the horses over; the profit is in the food and the liquor.'

Sarah asked what liquor was sold and he replied, 'We sell brandy, whisky and porter but also coffee.'

Sarah asked if it was so busy all the time and Roderick told her that it was, the coach from York stopped overnight and the passengers slept there and breakfast was provided for them. The breakfast consisted of pork pies, pickles, slices of baked ham and bread which Sarah thought was a substantial meal.

Roderick agreed, 'Travellers on the road have substantial appetites and we like to provide for them.'

Sarah said she would like to be shown round the inn so Roderick took her into the vaults where the passengers who rode on top of the coach were catered for. Sarah realized the difference between the first and second class passengers: if you rode on the outside of the coach, you were not offered such nice food as the passengers who rode on the inside! Roderick then took her into the kitchens where women were preparing food for the next coach. She then wanted to look at the cellars; Roderick took her down the stairs telling her to be careful of the steep steps. The cellars were long and narrow with a curved roof, all the wine was kept on one side and the barrels on the other. Sarah asked what was in the barrels and Roderick replied that the porter was kept on that side as it was cooler and the temperature was right. The maids bring a jug down to fill with the porter and fetch bottles of wine and brandy as needed. Sarah thought this was a world she did not know existed; she then asked to see the bedrooms.

They both went up the winding stairs, past an array of warming pans. Roderick said there were a dozen warming pans as there were a dozen bedrooms. The maids would fill them with hot coals to warm the beds as in the winter it was very cold. In the mornings, the maids would empty the chamber pots then they would be washed with lime and returned to the bedrooms. Sarah thought to herself this world of travel was a world of its own which, to Roderick's credit, all worked well.

She then said she would like to see the stables where the coach horses were. They were specially bred for the coach trade, York coach horses, seventeen hands and very strong so they could pull the coaches. Roderick told her there would be four or five changes of horses on a journey. He showed her the harness room, where the horses were harnessed ready for the journey. Sarah was intrigued by this world of travel; she had never seen anything like it. She told Roderick she thought it was a self-contained world and he replied that it was a world full of wheels and the wheels never stopped turning.

Sarah was proud of Roderick when she realised how he made his living, everything was clean, worked well and she thought the inn was in safe hands. When he asked her if she approved, she replied, 'Nearly,' and he laughed and said, 'You don't like the liquor.'

She replied, 'Maybe, maybe.'

Sarah felt her curiosity had at last been satisfied and she was very pleased to see how capably Roderick was running the inn.

Roderick asked Sarah if she would like some refreshments with him, she replied that she would so they sat down together in the parlour and enjoyed their meal. She had spent a lot of time in the inn and thought she should now make her way back to Cheswardine. Roderick arranged for Jess to be harnessed so they could make their way back home. Sarah felt she had achieved something this day and she had a deeper understanding of the work Roderick did and she was satisfied he was very capable at his task.

They made their way back to Cheswardine, the autumn had nearly gone and the winter was creeping in with a chill in the air. Roderick wrapped the rug round Sarah and she snuggled up to him as they made their way back home. Jess was trotting briskly along the country lanes in his eagerness to be home.

Roderick asked Sarah if she had thought of names for the child but she replied, 'I do not want to think of names at the minute. I want the birth to be over and then we will decide which name we will choose. Let us put it into God's hands and hope the birth goes well and then we will choose a name.' Roderick realised Sarah was right: get the birth over and then decide.

They snuggled together and enjoyed the ride back through the country lanes and soon saw the lights of Cheswardine. Abel was waiting for them as they pulled into the drive and he helped Sarah out of the trap and told them he would stable Jess.

They went inside and were glad to be home. A fire was burning in the grate in the library so they sat there for a while and reflected on what a perfect day they had enjoyed together.

CHAPTER 6

A Tragic Turn

It was soon the middle of December and the time was fast approaching for Sarah to give birth. One morning, she said to Emma that she thought it would be a good idea to send for Mrs Grace as the child was on its way. Emma went to the stables and told Abel to make haste and fetch Mrs Grace, as the baby's arrival was imminent. Abel went and picked Mrs Grace up from the village and returned quickly to Cheswardine.

Mrs Grace went straight into the library to speak with Sarah and, as they felt that the baby was ready to come, Sarah wanted someone to fetch Roderick from the inn, as he wanted to be in the house when the baby was born. Abel harnessed Jess once more and went to tell Roderick that the baby was on its way and he was needed back at home. Roderick wasted no time and informed the staff he would be returning to Cheswardine at once and gave a few instructions for things to be carried out in his absence. Abel waited for Roderick in the trap, then they set off back to Cheswardine with Jess trotting briskly, seeming to sense there was urgency to the trip.

Abel never used the whip on horses, he used kindness and gentleness to get the best out of animals as he had lived in the country all his life and he believed you achieved more with sugar than you do with vinegar. They went along the lanes and at last, Cheswardine came into sight, the lights were all on as Jess pulled up at the front door. Roderick said to Abel, 'You see to Jess and I will see you later.'

He bounded up the front steps and went inside, into the library where he found Sarah sitting in the big old armchair by the fire. Roderick asked if there was anything he could do to help but Sarah replied, 'Mrs Grace is here and preparing the bedroom. Birth is a thing women do best on their own and all you have to do when the baby is born is come and hold your new son or daughter.'

Sarah thought it was time for her to go to her bedroom, as she needed to lie down. Roderick kissed her and told her he would organise matters downstairs but Sarah told him everyone knew what to do and the best thing he could do was to relax in the library. He took this advice and tried to make himself busy in the library reading over documents.

When Mrs Grace came into the library and told Roderick all was well upstairs but there was still no sign of the baby, Roderick impressed upon her that he wanted to know as soon as there were any new developments.

Time went on, night arrived, and still there was no sign of the baby. Roderick was starting to feel very concerned about the situation. He asked to see Mrs Grace, when she came she told him there was no sign of the baby yet; first babies often took a long time and he was not to worry, the baby would come in its own time. The night went on, morning came and Mrs Grace was still confident so he asked if he could see Sarah. Mrs Grace told him he could so he went bounding up the stairs to see his wife. She was lying in bed and said, 'The baby is taking a long time to come but it will be worth the wait,' Roderick squeezed her hand and agreed. He returned to the library and continued the long wait.

The morning passed slowly and eventually, at about three o'clock in the afternoon, Mrs Grace came downstairs and told him the baby had been born, a lovely little girl and would he like to come upstairs and meet his new daughter. Roderick was so excited he took the stairs two at a time and rushed into the bedroom.

Sarah was sitting up holding the baby and Roderick thought he had never seen a prettier sight. He went to her and held her hand, gazed into her eyes and thanked her. He took his daughter in his arms and thought he had never seen such a beautiful baby, he squeezed Sarah's hand, they gazed into each other's eyes and there was no need for words.

Mrs Grace came bustling back and told him she needed to tidy Sarah up and shooed Roderick away. There was great happiness in the house at the birth of the baby and an atmosphere of joyous celebration. Roderick returned to the library and poured himself a celebration whisky.

After about half an hour, Mrs Grace came into the library in a rush and told Roderick she could not stop the bleeding and asked for plenty of hot towels to be sent up from the kitchen. Roderick began to feel very concerned at the situation; he went upstairs to see Sarah and asked her if she was going to be all right. Sarah assured him everything would be fine; Roderick went to the cot and gazed at his sleeping daughter.

Mrs Grace asked Roderick to send Emma up to him as she needed some help. Roderick told Emma who went running up the stairs. But Mrs Grace was unable to stop the bleeding, she had done everything she could, to no avail, the haemorrhaging would not stop. Mrs Grace told Emma the bed would need changing and more fresh towels applied and for them to tip the bed up at the feet. Emma did everything she was asked but Mrs Grace told

Emma she had never seen anyone bleed as much as Sarah and she thought Roderick should come upstairs.

Emma went to fetch Roderick who went straight to Sarah and held her hand. He told Mrs Grace he thought Sarah looked very pale and he thought they should send for the doctor and Mrs Grace agreed.

Sarah held onto Roderick's hand, looked into his eyes, and said to him, 'I want you to promise me you will look after the baby.' Roderick nodded and, as Sarah continued, 'I want to tell you, thank you for everything, you have made me very happy,' Roderick knew that she was slipping away.

Sarah held Roderick's hand very tightly and then suddenly the grip loosened, she gave a great sigh and Roderick knew he had lost her. He called Mrs Grace and she felt Sarah's pulse and told Roderick she had slipped away and there was nothing that could be done. Roderick was stunned and could not understand how this had happened; in a few short hours, Sarah had gone from him and he was the father of a baby girl.

He went downstairs, sat in the library, and tried to grasp the situation, which was so difficult. In a daze, he wandered into the kitchen, thinking life had dealt him a very cruel blow. A few hours ago, they had a wonderful future and now the future looked very black. Sorrow struck and Roderick could not cope with it, he did not know what to do, or how to cope with the situation. Sorrow is an uninvited and unwelcome guest, Roderick felt totally lost and bereft.

Abel had put Jess back in shafts and had gone to Chimneys to fetch Miss Charlotte as he thought she would help in the situation. Within half an hour, he arrived in the courtyard of Chimneys. When one of the grooms came over, Abel told him not to take Jess out of the shafts as the trap would be needed again more or less immediately. He went straight up the steps and knocked on the door.

When the maid answered, he told her it was very important that he saw Miss Charlotte immediately. She could see by Abel's face that some terrible event had occurred and she went straight to Miss Charlotte and Abel was ushered into the breakfast room where Miss Charlotte was sitting at the table.

Abel said, 'Madam, I am the bearer of bad news which I will try to break as gently as possible. Miss Sarah has passed away after the birth of a baby girl. Understandably, Mr Roderick is in a bad state and I wondered whether you could come and help with the situation.'

Miss Charlotte was stunned at the news and could not answer straight away, she could not comprehend the terrible news. She came from good stock and when situations arose she did not panic, so she pulled herself together and told Abel of course she would come. She was a very resourceful lady and was used to helping in difficult situations but never dreamed she would be called upon to help in something like this.

She called one of the maidservants and asked her to fetch Mr Torduff as she would like a word with him. A message was sent to the foundry and he came post-haste. He went straight to Charlotte and said, 'You would not have called me away on a trivial matter, I feel there is something very sad has happened.'

Charlotte replied, 'Sarah has passed away after childbirth. I would like you to come with me to Cheswardine to give our son some support.'

Both of them went to the front door where Abel was waiting with the trap to take them on their sad journey. Although they proceeded down the lanes at a fast pace, the journey seemed never ending but eventually they arrived at Cheswardine. Emma opened the door and said, 'Mr Roderick is still in the library.'

They made their way into the library and found Roderick sitting by the fire, his head in his hands. As soon as he saw his parents, he sobbed as if his heart would break. Like all mothers do, Charlotte had an inner strength in situations like this and clasped Roderick to her, holding him tightly. Meanwhile, Roderick's father looked on, unable to decide on the best thing to do as he felt overwhelmed by the grief around him. Charlotte held Roderick until he had cried himself into an exhausted state. Charlotte told him, 'We will cope and take the goodness out of a bad situation,' but Roderick could not understand the words. His whole world had dissolved and left him bereft so that he could comprehend nothing.

Miss Charlotte told Emma to make strong tea and bring it to them, and she would talk to Mr Roderick and try to see what could be done. Charlotte took Roderick's hand and said to him she understood he would need their help in this situation and he replied, 'Yes, Mother, I do, I feel incapable at this minute of making rational decisions.'

Charlotte hugged him and said, 'If you leave everything to me, I will make all necessary arrangements but you must try to cope with the situation. I know at this moment you cannot see any happiness but there is, you have a lovely daughter and she must take priority, Sarah would want you to do that. You will have to take the lead in raising your daughter as Sarah would have wished.'

Roderick understood that his mother spoke the truth and he was also aware of how evident the overwhelming love from mother to son was that day.

Miss Charlotte took the situation in hand and told Emma to ask Abel to go to Quaker Allen's and break the sad news to him and Sarah's mother and ask them to come over. With a heavy heart, Abel set off for Quaker Allen's home. When he arrived at the cottage and knocked on the door, Quaker Allen's wife herself answered. Abel asked if he could come in as he had some news for them. She invited Abel into the warm and welcoming room. When Abel asked if Quaker Allen was at home, she went and fetched her husband.

Abel was a shrewd man, he had lived many years and had gathered a lot of common sense along the way so he said to Quaker Allen:

'I think it would be better if we all sat down as I have some news for you. Unfortunately, I am the bearer of bad news, Sarah passed away after the birth of the baby, everything that could be done was done to save her life but it was not to be. I am so sorry to be the bearer of this bad news but she had a beautiful little girl who is very healthy. Miss Charlotte is at Cheswardine and she would like you to go over and discuss with her all the arrangements as, naturally, she thought it was only correct to consult you.'

Quaker Allen sat at the table trying to gather his thoughts. He said, 'It is a terrible thing to see your children die before you. It should not have been this way.' He looked at his wife and said, 'We must try to cope with this situation as I feel we have no alternative.' Quaker Allen fetched his coat, his wife fetched her shawl, and they went to the trap with Abel.

When they arrived at Cheswardine, Emma opened the door and told them Miss Charlotte was waiting for them in the library. They went into the library and Miss Charlotte offered them refreshments which they declined. She then told them Roderick was terribly shocked and was not coping well with the situation and he had asked his mother to organise everything.

Charlotte asked Quaker Allen for his advice and he replied that he thought Sarah would like to be buried in the Quaker plot in the churchyard, where he and his wife would eventually be buried. Charlotte agreed with this arrangement and suggested the funeral should be in a week's time and she would arrange the time with the sexton. She made other suggestions for the day but Quaker Allan had no fight left in him: he had lost his favourite daughter and agreed with her arrangements. However, he did say that he wished to make the casket for Sarah, as the one final service he could do for his daughter.

The day of the funeral dawned. The house was full of sorrow; not even the birth of the baby had brought any joy. The coffin was to be set on a farmer's dray, pulled by two black horses with plumes on their heads and two dark blankets over them. The farmers' wives had picked what greenery they could from the countryside and strewn it around the bed of the dray upon which the coffin would sit. The men of the estate gently carried the coffin out of the house and placed it in the middle of the bed of the dray. As was the custom, all the farm labourers wore clean white smocks and their wives wore their Sunday best. They all stood behind the dray and waited for the family to come out. Abel had brought Jess out without the trap but in full harness to walk behind the dray as he thought the horse should join the procession; he said Jess would want to say goodbye too. Animals seem to know when sorrow is about, Jess was quite restless, and Abel had difficulties in controlling him.

Quaker Allan had been in his garden that morning and picked some sprays of flowering shrubs. As the coffin was carried through the main entrance, he stepped forward and placed them on the coffin. The family followed as the coffin was placed on the trap and then they climbed into the coaches. Roderick's mother and father escorted him and his brother Daniel, while Quaker Allen and his family followed in the second coach. The household staff followed on foot behind the coaches, Emma, Polly and the housemaids following the dray.

They set off on their mournful journey to the Quakers' meetinghouse. The dray passed through the beautiful countryside where Sarah had lived all her life, this was her last journey and the trees seemed to bend their branches as she passed and the rabbits paused in their games to watch. When they arrived at the meetinghouse, the elder Quaker greeted them and the coffin was taken inside. Roderick and the family followed, all the Quakers were present but, as there was not enough room for all staff from the house, they stood outside in silence.

The elder Quaker said, 'Welcome everyone on this sad occasion. Sarah was not on this earth very long but she made her mark. She made her husband, Roderick, very happy and all the people she came into contact with. We must now we say farewell to Sarah and remember all the happy times.'

Weeping could be heard but Roderick stood stony-faced as the men from the estate lifted the coffin, and bore it out of the meetinghouse to the Quaker area in the cemetery. The families followed, then the household staff, then the outdoor staff and people from the surrounding area who had come to pay their last respects to Sarah. The elder Quaker stood at the head of the coffin and said, 'We all say goodbye to Sarah and thank her for the memories she has left behind.'

The ceremony was over and Roderick seemed to give up at that stage; his mother went across to support him. She told him she would come back to Cheswardine with him for a time, as she thought he should not be on his own. If there is such a thing as a broken heart, Roderick's was breaking.

She led him back to the coach and they set off for Cheswardine. The black trappings were removed from the cart and Emma, Polly and the household staff rode on the dray back to the house.

When Miss Charlotte and Roderick arrived home, they went straight into the library where a fire burned brightly in the grate. Emma arrived and Miss Charlotte told her she would like a word with her after they had all had a cup of tea. Roderick was given a cup of strong tea, the fire was replenished and Roderick sat by the fire, silently drinking his tea.

Miss Charlotte went into the kitchen to speak to Emma; she asked if Emma was prepared to look after the baby, if not, a wet nurse from the village could be hired. Emma told Miss Charlotte she would be happy to care for the baby as she had a lot of experience with younger brothers and sisters. Miss Charlotte was pleased and told her she was happy to be putting her granddaughter in safe hands. She felt she had made the right decision in the light of the circumstances. Miss Charlotte stayed on at Cheswardine for a few days to support Roderick until she was satisfied he seemed to be on an even keel then she left to return to Chimneys.

CHAPTER 7

More Family Loss

Time went on and Roderick seemed to sink deeper into gloom but, eventually, one day he sent for Abel and said, 'It is time I went back to the inn as I need to check how things are being run. I would like you to keep an eye on the estate. You know how things are run and you have been here all your working life.'

Abel replied that he would do his best as he felt he owed it to Sarah and Roderick to keep things going. Roderick had a word with Emma and told her that if she needed extra help in the house she was to arrange it as he knew having a newborn baby in the house would make extra work. Emma said they were managing well and she was enjoying looking after Elizabeth. Roderick looked surprised as he did not even know the name of the baby but Emma told him Miss Sarah had wanted the baby to be called Elizabeth and that is how the staff had come to know her. Roderick accepted this as life had seemed to be a fog since Sarah had died and he had given the child hardly any thought.

Next morning, Abel saddled Bluebell and Roderick went to the inn. As he rode along he realised this was the beginning of his life without Sarah and he wondered how he was going to cope.

When he arrived at the inn, it was very busy as usual, as it was on the main London road with coaches arriving all the time. He walked around organising things that had slid in his absence and the day passed quickly with many things to think about until evening came and Roderick sent for his horse and made his way home.

It was a dark, stormy night but Bluebell knew her way home and they made their way safely back along the roads until they saw the lights of Cheswardine. Roderick dismounted and as he did so there was the sound of breaking glass, a bottle of brandy had fallen from his saddlebag. He had the presence of mind to make sure Bluebell did not step on the glass and called out for Abel to fetch her. He then reached into his saddlebag and, as he took the other bottle of brandy out, fell heavily. Abel arrived and, as soon as he saw Roderick struggling to stand, realised that he had been drinking. He escorted Roderick into the house and sat him in the library, then left to take Bluebell to the stable, telling Mr Roderick he would return when she had been settled for the night.

Abel took Bluebell into the stable, rubbed her down, fed her, gave her clean water, and settled her down. When he returned via the kitchens to Roderick in the library, he was still sitting there, in front of the fire with a bottle of brandy in one hand and his riding crop in the other. He asked Abel whether Bluebell was all right and Abel replied, 'Yes she is fine, but are you alright, Mr Roderick?'

Roderick replied wearily, 'Maybe.'

Emma had prepared his supper and Abel asked Roderick where he would like to eat it, in the dining room or the kitchen. Roderick just wanted to sit in the library and gather his thoughts. Abel looked at Roderick and said, 'Beg pardon, Sir, I have known you since you were a small boy and I hope I am not speaking out of turn, but I do feel you should make an effort to eat some supper after a hard day's work.'

'I could not eat a thing, I do appreciate your concern but I have no appetite.' He then poured himself another glass of brandy and gazed into the fire.

Abel shook his head, returned to the kitchen, and said to Emma, 'I don't think he is going to find happiness in the brandy bottle, it is not the solution to anything. I think the situation is getting worse. I thought having Elizabeth in the house would bring a lot of joy but it has not; the house is now burdened with sorrow.'

After a while, Emma went into the library to see if Roderick was still awake but he was fast asleep, with the empty brandy bottle on the floor. Emma went and fetched a travelling rug and covered Roderick over, the only thing she could do for him. Emma locked the house up and went upstairs to settle the child; Elizabeth slept in her room in the cot made by her Quaker grandfather. She was a beautiful child, with blonde hair and blue eyes. Emma knew she wanted to take care of the baby as she had bonded with Miss Sarah and had loved her dearly, and she felt this was a way she could repay all the kindness that Sarah had shown her.

In the following weeks, Roderick went to the inn each day and returned to Cheswardine where he spent the night drinking brandy until he fell into a stupor. The situation was worsening, both Emma and Abel were very worried but felt helpless to rectify matters. Abel was working hard to keep things running outside and Emma was doing all she could in running the house and looking after Elizabeth, but both of them felt the situation was out of control. Roderick had gone to pieces and was drinking a bottle of brandy a night, he took no interest in Elizabeth at all, his only interest was the brandy bottle.

One evening he arrived home with one of the ladies from the inn. They sat in the library, drinking brandy together, and when Emma asked if would he like supper, he replied, 'No, I have good company and the brandy and that will suffice.' Emma returned to the kitchen thinking the situation was very grave, but this state of affairs continued over the next month, with the woman staying at Cheswardine and starting to take over the running of the house. She was very abrupt with the staff and did not seek permission to change things. Eventually, Emma confronted her one day and said she was in charge of the house and she would decide how things were to be run. The woman replied that she, Jane, was Roderick's common-law wife and would now be taking over and would decide how the household would be run so Emma should do as she was told. Emma replied she would never be the lady of the house as that had been Miss Sarah's position and nobody could replace her.

Great unhappiness spread throughout the house, Roderick was searching for something that he could never find. Jane could never replace Sarah: drink was in and wit was out. Roderick would arrive each night from the inn with his customary bottle of brandy and make his way to the library.

One night, it was very cold and Emma went round closing all the shutters to try to keep the heat in. Roderick did not want any supper but sat drinking his brandy with Jane at his side, also drinking. Emma left them alone and went to bed.

The next morning she was awakened by terrible screaming. Jane ran up the stairs screaming for Emma, 'Roderick is dead.'

Emma ran down the stairs as fast as she could into the library and there was Mr Roderick slumped on one side of the armchair and two empty bottles on the floor. Emma felt for a pulse but she knew he was dead. She sent for Abel and told him to go over to Chimneys, tell Miss Charlotte what had happened and ask her to come straight away. Within two hours, Miss Charlotte arrived at Cheswardine and went straight to the library where Roderick was still in the chair. She asked Abel to fetch the outside men to move Mr Roderick and take him to his bedroom. Roderick was carried upstairs and laid in his bedroom.

Miss Charlotte then turned to Jane and said, 'I would like you to leave Cheswardine as your presence here is no longer needed, you have done great harm to this family.'

Jane replied, 'I have no intention of leaving; I am Roderick's common-law wife and now I am his widow. I shall be staying here and claiming my rights.'

Miss Charlotte looked at her and said, 'There is nothing here that belongs to you, only the unhappiness you have brought into this house. You have brought only liquor and sorrow. We have nothing to thank you for and the best thing you can do is pack your belongings and go.'

But Jane still refused to go and said she would claim what was rightfully hers. Miss Charlotte replied, 'That will never be but there are more pressing things to do than bandy words with you.'

Miss Charlotte then said to Emma she would come and help her lay Mr Roderick out. Emma fetched water and towels, washed Roderick and put him in his good suit. Both of them felt great sorrow at the task they were performing as, such a short time ago, the whole house was filled with happiness and now the weight of sorrow bore everyone down. Miss Charlotte was a strong character, she had plenty of stamina and she coped with the situation with fortitude and courtesy as she helped Emma perform this last service for Roderick.

When the task was completed they went downstairs to Jane and Miss Charlotte repeated that it was in her best interest to leave Cheswardine. She was prepared to give her a small amount of money to start her new life. Again, Jane told Miss Charlotte she had no intention of leaving and would not be bribed, but she was entitled to some of the estate. Miss Charlotte reiterated that would never be and told her, 'I am going back to Chimneys and will return in two days when I expect you to be gone.' So saying she marched from the room.

Miss Charlotte made her way back to Chimneys with a heavy heart. On the way back she thought about the past and how Roderick was as a young boy, remembering him with his lovely blond hair and blue eyes, a true Nordic child. As her memories flooded in, so did the sorrow and tears and she sobbed all the way back to Chimneys, as mothers do when they lose a child.

'Happiness seems to have forsaken us. I have lost my lovely son and my beautiful daughter-in-law,' she thought.

These thoughts went through her mind, but being the strong, determined character she was, she then went on to think what must be done next. The immediate thing to concentrate on would be Roderick's funeral which would be a great sadness but then she needed to plan her granddaughter's future. So many thoughts were passing through her mind as she drove back to Chimneys, she had a heavy heart and felt weighed down with sorrow.

As she arrived back at Chimneys, one of the grooms came out and took the halter of the horse. Miss Charlotte said, 'I would like you fetch Mr Torduff and Daniel from the foundy as I need to see them immediately. It is very important.'

The groom knew by her voice that a great tragedy had occurred. Miss Charlotte went up the steps and into the hall and made her way to the sitting room where a bright fire was burning. She stood in front of the fire warming herself as she felt cold after the shock and the journey.

Her husband arrived and said, 'I understand you want to see me.'

Charlotte replied, 'Yes, but I need Daniel to be here too as this sadness is almost too much to bear.' Her husband immediately realised something terrible had happened.

When Daniel came into the room and greeted his mother, Charlotte looked at them, saying, 'I think you had both better sit down, as I am the bearer of dreadful news. I have been over to Cheswardine this morning and Roderick is dead. He has a woman called Jane there who is claiming to be his common-law wife: she is making a claim on the estate, so we have two burdens to carry. We have to bury our son and your brother, which is a great sadness to all of us. The other burden is this Jane woman, who used to work at the inn. As a family, we need to find the best solution to this problem.'

Daniel, who had never been eloquent, said, 'Well, Mother, you are, indeed, the bearer of bad news. I have lost a brother and I have lost a lovely sister-in-law, it has not been a good time for us. We will have to make the best of these circumstances, the only good thing to come out of all this is that you have a lovely granddaughter and you can build a life round her.'

His mother nodded and said, 'We will need to build one step at a time to see what we are going to do.'

Old Mr Torduff said, 'It will be difficult to get rid of Jane, but she has no legal claim to the estate or any of its assets.' He thought the best thing to do would be to get in touch with the High Sheriff of the county, explain the position to him, that they had somebody would not vacate the estate and ask for his advice. Charlotte agreed and said she would send a message to him.

Charlotte then said, 'Firstly, the most important thing we have to do is to organise the funeral for Roderick.'

Her husband replied, 'It is a very sad thing when we have to organise a funeral for our son, it is not the natural order of life.'

Charlotte agreed with him, 'It should not be this way round but it has happened and we need to deal with the situation. I think Roderick should be buried in a plot in the Quaker cemetery with Sarah so they can be together.'

Father and son agreed this was the correct thing to do and Charlotte said she would get in touch with Quaker Allen about the service and burial.

The next morning Charlotte sent for a groom and told him to harness the pony and trap then asked one of the coachmen to take her to Quaker Allen's cottage. The horse and trap was brought around to the front door, Miss Charlotte climbed up into it and they made their way to Quaker Allen's cottage. It was still winter, the morning was cold and Miss Charlotte grew cold during the drive despite the warm blanket covering her. They arrived at the cottage and, as they pulled up outside, she asked the groom to wait for her. If the pony became cold he should cover her with a rug, the coachman nodded and knew she cared for her animals.

Charlotte walked up the path to the cottage. It was a well-tended house and garden and she knew this home had been cared for with love. She knocked at the door; Quaker Allen's wife opened the door and looked startled to see Miss Charlotte standing there.

Charlotte said, 'I am Miss Charlotte and I have come from Chimneys.'

Quaker Allen's wife replied, 'Yes, of course, please come in.'

As Charlotte entered, she asked, 'Is Quaker Allen available as I have some news for you and I would prefer to tell you both at the same time as the news I have to impart is not good.'

Mrs Allen replied, 'Yes, I will go and fetch him, he is milking the cows.'

She went outside to her husband and said, 'Miss Charlotte is here from Chimneys and I think there is some sorrow on the way.' He gave the cow some straw to chew on and followed his wife back into the house.

Charlotte said, 'I am afraid I am the bearer of bad news. We have had some sorrow in this family and there is more now to come. Roderick, my son, died two nights ago and I have come here to ask you if it would be possible to bury him with Sarah so they can be together.'

Quaker Allen and his wife were stunned by the news and he sat down heavily. His wife came to sit by him and held his hand. Charlotte said the funeral would be in a week's time and she would like them both to come with their daughters. Quaker Allen replied with tears in his eyes, as the funeral of his daughter was still fresh in his mind, 'Yes, we will all come.' He felt the overwhelming sorrow of losing both young people was almost too much to bear.

Miss Charlotte asked Quaker Allen if he could arrange for the plot to be opened and he agreed. The funeral would take place in one week; the funeral procession would leave from Cheswardine and make their way to the Quaker burial ground. Quaker Allen asked Charlotte if she wanted a ceremony at her church, or if she wanted the funeral procession to go straight to the Quaker burial ground.

Miss Charlotte thought for a moment and said, 'When Roderick and Sarah married, the arrangement was that he would become a Quaker so we will stick to that and he will be buried as a Quaker as Sarah would have wanted.'

The old Quaker looked at her and thought what a gracious lady she was, she managed to keep her dignity even with all her sorrow around her. Charlotte then said, 'If you will forgive me, I must make my way back to Chimneys as there are a lot of arrangements to make.'

She made her way back to the trap where the coachman assisted her and wrapped the rug around her, as the day had become colder and he thought it might snow. They set off and snow did begin to fall. The coachman said, 'It looks like we still have some harsh weather to come this winter,' but Charlotte did not reply as she was too engrossed with her sad thoughts.

They made their way back to Chimneys; once they reached the main entrance, the coachman halted the trap and helped Miss Charlotte alight. She went into the house where Daniel was waiting for her and told her they had a visitor, he was from the office of the High Sheriff and would like a word. Charlotte and Daniel went into the sitting room and greeted the gentleman standing by the fire. He told them he had received their message and had come to see what the problem was. Charlotte offered the gentleman some refreshment but he asked her just to apprise him of the situation so he could try to be of assistance.

'My son Roderick, who has recently died, had an association with one of the ladies from the inn which he owned. She spent a couple of months at Cheswardine and is now making a claim on the estate as the common-law wife of my son.'

The officer said he would look into the situation, but from the information Miss Charlotte had given him and as far as he knew, she would have no claim. He then asked Miss Charlotte when she would next be going to Cheswardine. When she told him she would be going over in the morning to make arrangements for her son's funeral, the officer asked, if it was convenient with Miss Charlotte, could he escort her to Cheswardine and try to expedite the matter sooner rather than later. Miss Charlotte appreciated the offer and thought it was the right thing to do so arrangements were made for the officer to arrive at Chimneys at ten o'clock the next morning.

The following morning, the Sheriff arrived promptly at ten o'clock and they set off for Cheswardine. The morning was cold and there was a light covering of snow on the ground. The cold seeped into their bones and Charlotte and the Sheriff were pleased of the blankets over their legs. The journey took about an hour and, as they entered the gates, the drive was covered in snow. The only evidence of habitation was the prints of rabbits and other animals in the snow.

Despite being a large house, Cheswardine gave the impression of homeliness; Abel was waiting for them at the main entrance and helped Miss Charlotte down. He touched his cap, greeted her, and told her he was pleased to see her. Miss Charlotte smiled and squeezed his hand. She introduced the Sheriff to Abel and explained, 'The Sheriff has come to advise us on the situation we find ourselves in.' They all walked into the hall where Emma was waiting to greet them.

'Good morning, Emma,' Miss Charlotte responded. 'Would you tell Jane we would like a word with her, we will go into the library. Please bring some coffee as the journey has chilled us.'

Emma went to fetch Jane and Miss Charlotte and the Sheriff warmed themselves by the fire as they waited.

Jane arrived in the library, 'I believe you wanted to speak to me?'

The Sheriff looked at her, 'Are you Jane? And what is your surname?'

'My surname is Hardcourt,' Jane replied.

'Are you a spinster, married or a widow?' the Sheriff asked.

Jane replied, drawing herself up to her full height, 'I am the common-law wife of Roderick.'

'That is make believe,' he replied, 'You are not the common law wife of Roderick. You are making a false claim, which is an offence, and I advise you to vacate these premises and, if you do not leave, you will be summoned to attend the magistrates' court. In this particular case, you could be deported to Australia. My advice to you is to pack your belongings and leave Cheswardine in the morning and all these threats will be forgotten.'

Miss Charlotte could see that Jane was frightened at the thought of prosecution and being sent to Australia by the Magistrate. The Sheriff knew his job and would have carried the threat to completion. Charlotte thought the situation had been dealt with well and Jane would be gone in the morning. Jane left the library without another word. Miss Charlotte and the Sheriff drank their coffee and then made their way back to Chimneys after saying goodbye to Emma.

They arrived at Chimneys and the groom helped Miss Charlotte to alight. The Sheriff asked Miss Charlotte if there were any other problems she would like him to attend to but she said there were not. She asked him if he would like some refreshments before commencing his journey but he replied, 'No thank-you, the sky is full of snow. I would prefer to go on my way before the weather breaks and the light goes because once the snow starts falling in these parts it does not stop.'

Miss Charlotte shook his hand and said, 'Thank-you for all your help in this matter. It has all been very painful, we have had an abundance of sorrow to bear and this matter has made it worse.'

The Sheriff replied, 'I appreciate that. If you have any more trouble at Cheswardine, please inform us and we will give you every possible assistance.' He then touched his hat, mounted his horse and set off on his return journey.

As Miss Charlotte went up the steps to the house she felt glad to be home. She went straight into the sitting room and warmed herself by the fire as the winter cold was fierce. She sat in the sitting room, mulling over the situation and Daniel arrived and came in to see her and ask how the situation was progressing. She told him she hoped it had been resolved, Jane knew her position, and she would be leaving in the morning. This would please everyone when she goes.

Daniel smiled, 'Yes, it will, if she goes. How are the funeral arrangements progressing?'

Charlotte replied, 'I have seen Quaker Allen and all the arrangements are in place for the service and burial. It is just the other arrangements to be finalised and then everything is set. The only other question is about Cheswardine, somebody has to go and live there and organise the running of the estate and I wondered if you would be interested.'

Daniel looked at her with surprise, 'The foundry is busy at the moment, but if you want me to go to Cheswardine for a few days I will willingly go. But, in the long term, Mother, it is your family home and I know you would never want to sell it as there are a lot of memories there, a lot of happiness, and I am sure you would like to keep the house.'

Charlotte replied, 'Yes, I would like to keep it, so I think the long-term solution would be to put in a bailiff to run the estate. Sarah had put in a lot of work to make the estate a viable proposition and it would be wrong to waste that.'

Daniel agreed that would be the best solution and he would supervise Cheswardine for now while they sought a bailiff.

Back at Cheswardine, Jane had decided to go the following morning, as she had been frightened into realising she had no rights to the estate or any claim to it. However, she was determined not to go unrewarded; she would take some of the silver and any other small items she could sell. She packed her belongings ready to leave the following morning from the crossroads, on the coach going to Brampton. Unbeknown to Emma, she had been round the house, removing small items she thought were of value which, in her mind, she considered as payment for the services she had rendered. Everything was packed ready for the morning.

At six o'clock the next morning, she was ready to leave to catch the coach when, at the last minute, she decided she would take the baby with her as a final act of revenge. She crept into the nursery, wrapped the baby in a shawl and blanket and made her way to the crossroads with the rest of her ill-gotten gains. The morning was bitterly cold and, as she stood waiting for the coach, the baby began to cry. Jane wrapped the baby more tightly in the blankets and rocked her until she stopped crying.

The sound of the coach horn could be heard as it approached the cross roads to warn the waiting passengers the coach was on its way. When it arrived, the coachman asked Jane where she was bound and, when she said she was going to Brampton, he told her the fare would be four shillings. Jane paid him and stepped into the coach; inside she found another traveller who was asleep. Jane settled herself and the baby down and the coach set off.

There was a lot of snow on the way and the weather was becoming colder. The baby started to cry and woke the other passenger; the woman asked Jane if the baby needed feeding and she told her no, she did not, she was just fretful. Jane rocked the baby until she fell asleep again. The coach took about an hour and a half to reach Brampton.

On arrival, as she was leaving the coach, Jane asked the coachman if he knew of a place where she could sell some trinkets. He told her of a place called Callums on the High Street and gave her directions. She made her way carefully as the High Street was covered in snow and carrying the baby and all her belongings made for a hazardous journey.

She found Callums, a small shop with a bow window displaying clocks and other pieces of value. She went in and asked the man behind the counter if he would be interested in buying the trinkets she wanted to sell. He wanted to see them so she set her bundle on the floor and took out the items she had removed from Cheswardine; small silver ornaments, silver letter openers, snuffboxes, picture frames and even some jewellery she had found of Sarah's. The jeweller looked at them carefully and told Jane they were good quality silver but asked her how she had come by them. Jane answered, 'They were gifts from my late husband. I have no further use for them as I am moving away from the area to start a new life.'

He looked at her and said, 'I will give you two guineas for them,' but Jane replied, 'That is not enough.'

The jeweller would not be moved and said, 'Take it or leave it, yes or no?'

As Jane decided she would have to take the offer, the baby started to cry. The jeweller asked her if the baby was all right and did it need feeding but, again, Jane said she was fine, just to give her the two guineas and she could be on her way quickly. The jeweller went to his cash drawer and gave her the two guineas; she put the money safely in her purse and left the shop.

Jane went out to the High Street and the baby began to cry even more. She saw an inn and went in to buy some food and feed the baby. The inn was small with low ceilings; there was a long room with a large fireplace at the end, with an open fire burning. As Jane sat near the fire, warming herself, one of the women of the inn came and asked if she could help and would she like something to eat. She offered cooked ham, pickles and fresh bread which Jane replied would be fine, then the woman asked her if the baby was all right, as it was crying a lot. Jane agreed it was crying a lot but was just fretful.

When the woman brought her food she asked if she could help with the baby, as the continual crying indicated the baby was hungry. She asked Jane if she was the mother and Jane replied that she was not: it was her sister's but she had died and she was now taking care of the baby. The woman told her she had many children, she thought the baby needed feeding and, if she could not feed her herself, she would be better off taking the child to the workhouse where they had wet nurses and could feed the baby. Jane asked where the workhouse was and the woman told her it was the large building at the end of the street and, if she rang the bell, assistance would be given.

Jane made her way along the street; it was still snowing and very cold. As she reached the workhouse and rang the doorbell, the baby was still crying. The door was opened by a lady who asked, 'What can we do for you?'

Jane replied, 'The baby needs feeding. I am not the mother, she has died but the child needs help.'

The woman ushered her into a room and asked what the child's name was and Jane replied, 'Her name is Elizabeth.' Then the woman asked her if the child was a foundling but Jane assured her the child was her sister's who had recently died. The woman told Jane to leave the baby and the child would be admitted to the workhouse to be looked after. Jane turned and walked through the door back onto the High Street, leaving Elizabeth in the workhouse.

The woman fetched the Chief Beadle and told him another infant had been admitted and a wet nurse was required quickly as the baby needed feeding. The Beadle fetched one of the wet nurses and told her the baby needed a good feed. As the wet nurse picked the baby up, she noticed a lovely necklace round the child's neck. She pointed this out to the Beadle and told him she thought the baby had come from a good home. The Beadle told the wet nurse to leave the necklace on the baby and he would book the baby in as Elizabeth Foundling as somebody would want a girl and give her a good upbringing. Meanwhile, Jane had gone to the centre of the town to catch a coach out of Brockton, to another destination.

CHAPTER 8

Lost and Found

At Cheswardine, when Emma woke and went into the nursery to fetch the baby, she saw the empty cot and realised the baby had gone. Panic-stricken, she rushed throughout the house, then went out to Abel and told him the baby was missing. Abel said, 'I think, in revenge and nastiness, Jane has taken the baby. She is a very nasty lady and the more she practises the nastier she gets. The best thing I can do is to go to Chimneys and give Miss Charlotte the news that the baby has been abducted and ask her to get in touch with the Sheriff to organise a search.'

Emma was not satisfied with this as she wanted to look for the baby herself. She went down into the yard and asked one of the farm workers if they had seen Jane. The man told her yes, he had seen her very early that morning walking to the crossroads with the baby. Emma understood at once that Jane had caught the coach to Brockton and taken the baby with her.

She went back to the house and up to Jane's room: there was nothing there at all. She then went to the dining room and saw that some of the smaller pieces of silver had gone; Jane had taken them too, out of revenge. Emma decided she would catch the coach to Brockton and follow her. She went upstairs and fetched her heavy cloak with the hood then set off down the lane to the crossroads, as she knew there was a coach that left at one o'clock.

She arrived early at the crossroads, it was a very cold day and Emma knew the journey would be arduous. She heard the coach in the distance and, when it arrived, she asked if she could sit inside. She paid her fare; she was the only one on the coach as the weather was so bad nobody wanted to travel. It took about one and a half hours to Brockton and, when she arrived, she asked the coachman where someone could sell silver trinkets. He told her there was a little shop on the High Street so she walked up the street and found the shop. Sure enough, when she looked in the window, she recognised all the trinkets from the house.

Emma went into the shop and said to the shopkeeper, 'Sir, please could you help me?' He told her, if he could, he would. Emma asked him where the pieces of silver had come from. The man told her a lady had come in earlier with a small baby and said they were the property of her deceased sister. Emma told him that was not correct and she had stolen them from Cheswardine, but she told him she was not interested in the trinkets. She wanted to know where the woman had taken the baby so the man told her he had seen her walking down the street and, at a calculated guess, she was going to the inn. Emma thanked him, went along to the inn, and sat down.

When the woman innkeeper came over to her, Emma asked if she had seen a woman with a baby. The woman told her there had been a woman that morning with a baby that needed feeding. Emma asked if she knew where she was and the woman told her she thought she had taken her to the workhouse.

With no more ado, Emma went back out to the High Street and went to the workhouse, where she rang the bell. A woman opened the door and Emma asked her if she had taken any babies in that morning. The woman told her they had taken a little girl in that morning, a blue-eyed, blonde-haired baby and they had just given her a feed. Emma asked if she could come in and the woman let her in. She told her the baby belonged to her and she would like her back. The woman told her she would have to fetch the Beadle; when he came, he explained the rules of the workhouse were that a payment had to be made of two guineas for a boy and one guinea for a girl and she would have to pay to get the child back. Emma said, 'Sir, all I have is one guinea,' but the beadle was adamant that it was one guinea if she wanted the baby. He rang the bell and a woman appeared.

He said, 'The foundling we had this morning?'

'Elizabeth?' and the Beadle said, 'That's the baby.'

When the woman fetched the baby, the joy in Emma's face was unbelievable. She had formed a bond with Elizabeth as she had with her mother and she had come a long way to find the baby. Fate and luck had been in her favour and brought her to the workhouse and all she wanted to do now was hold the baby in her arms.

The Beadle told her he would make a bill out for her for the infant that had been brought to the workhouse only that morning. He did so and wrote a receipt for one guinea; Emma opened her purse and gave him the guinea, which was all the money she had.

Emma then asked him, 'The baby always wears a necklace from her mother,' to which he replied, Yes, if you look, it is still round her neck. She came with it and she goes with it. Now, the weather looks like there is going to be a blizzard. Where are you heading?'

Emma replied, 'I am going to take the baby straight home.' She thought this baby has lost her mother and then her father and, for a short time, she had lost the baby; she was not going to let that happen again. She decided she was going to take the baby back to her home and raise it as her child, she had bonded with her and she was never going to let her out of sight again.

She collected the baby, wrapped herself in her cloak, put the hood up, and tucked the baby inside her cloak to keep her warm. Emma walked down the High Street towards the Great North Road to take the baby to her home.

As she walked along, she met a man who asked her where she was heading and she told him North Staffordshire. The man said, 'That is over two hundred miles. You will never get there. It is going to be a bad night and you will never make it.' Emma thanked him for his advice, but carried on walking along the Great North Road. As she walked, the snow began to fall heavily and the wind began to blow.

She had got about two miles from Brampton when, in the distance, she heard the coaching horn and she knew the coach was coming along the road towards her. It passed her but the coachman pulled up the four great horses and stopped just in front of her. The assistant coachman got down, came towards her and said, 'It's a very bad night to be out, where are you heading for?'

Emma told him, 'I am heading for North Staffordshire.'

The coachman told her she would not get that far tonight as the weather was getting worse. They were heading for the inn about ten miles down the road where the horses were being taken off the road to rest; they would be stopping at the inn until the blizzard was over.

The coachman said, 'There are no seats inside but you are welcome to ride on the top for free.' Emma thanked him and gratefully took him up on his offer.

She undid her cloak and passed the baby to the assistant coachman as she clambered aboard, then he handed her the baby and told her to wrap herself up in her cloak and a blanket he had given her as it was going to be a cold night. The assistant coachman returned to his seat and they set off.

The wind blew stronger and the weather grew colder, the horses started to pant as the snow fell more heavily and covered the road more thickly. After a while, the under coachman got down onto the road as the horses could not see where to go so he began to lead them; they were moving at a very slow pace as the snow was getting deeper and the blizzard worse.

The coachman stopped the horse and said to his assistant, 'We will not get much farther. The snow is getting thicker and the horses won't go much farther if it comes up to their stomachs. There is the George Inn half a mile down the road, I think we should stop there and wait for the blizzard to pass.'

They agreed on this plan and the under coachman led the horses as they struggled to move forward. This was one of the worst winters for many years. As luck would have it, they soon saw the lights of the George Inn.

The ostlers came out and told them there would be no change of horses tonight as further up the road it was three feet deep in snow and nothing could get through. The coachman understood and asked him to take the horses out of the shafts and give them a good rub down, as there was a lot of snow and ice on the harnesses. They unhitched the horses and took them into the stables.

Then the coachman opened the coach door and told the passengers there was no way they could carry on as the weather was too bad, they would have to stay the night at the inn but there was a good warm fire, good food and they would have to make the best of a bad job. 'We will stop here tonight and see what tomorrow brings,' he said and they all went into the inn.

Emma was still on top of the coach, completely covered in snow. The coachman shouted up, 'Madam, we are stopping here tonight as the coach can go no further. Come down and take shelter in the inn.'

There was no reply. The coachman climbed onto the coach and shook Emma. Still no reply. He pulled her hood down and realised why there had been no response. Emma was dead. They opened the cloak and found the baby still alive but Emma had perished from the cold and total exhaustion.

The coachman called the innkeeper and told him a lady had died on top of the coach but there was a baby that was still alive. They took Emma off the coach and gently laid her on the ground, then took the baby into the inn. The innkeeper's wife came to help and agreed it was a tragedy but it would not be the first time that somebody died of cold and exhaustion on the outside of a coach. The coachman asked her what they should do with the body until the roads were passable again. The innkeeper's wife said it would be better to put Emma in the corn store until they could get in touch with the clerk of the Parish Council and inform him of the death. The coachmen and the ostlers went out and carried Emma into the corn store. There was nothing else they could do; the sorrow went all round the inn, the only light in the sadness being that the baby had survived. There is nothing like a young baby to bring happiness and all the people in the inn looked at the baby and marvelled at the miracle that had kept her alive.

The travellers from the coach huddled round the fire and the innkeeper shut all the shutters to keep the snow and wind out. The innkeeper's wife laid on food for the travellers in the saloon where they were welcome to help themselves. Some of them availed themselves of the hospitality but others sat round the fire just pleased to feel warm again; it had been a nasty experience and they were pleased of the warmth and shelter. One of the passengers was holding the baby; the innkeeper's wife, Meg Jolly, asked if she could hold her a while. She and her husband, Winton, had three sons and one daughter but Meg had always wanted another daughter. Looking at the baby, she thought God had given her another chance of a daughter. She nursed the baby; she was a very pretty child.

The snow lasted for over a week; the ostler walked along the road and reported back that the Great North Road was still blocked so all they could do was wait for the weather to improve. Fortunately, the inn had plenty of food and was self-sufficient with eggs from the chickens and milk from their cows. The inn's storeroom had plenty of supplies for all the travellers and there was no shortage of kindness towards them either. They were held hostage by the weather; unable to continue their journeys until it improved.

In the meantime, Meg had developed a strong bond with the baby and taken to the child as if she were her own, as some women do with a young baby. One night she said to Winton that she was not going to bed but would sit in the chair by the fire, she was going to put the baby in a drawer by the fire as it was very cold in the bedroom and she thought the child would be warmer there. Her husband told her that he was happy for her to do what was necessary; it was all right by him. Every night through the coldest weather, Meg slept in the chair with the baby by her side, deepening the bond that had already formed.

Meg said to her husband she thought they should notify the Parish clerk of Emma's death, so a burial could be arranged. Winton agreed with her that it should be done, as soon as someone could get through the snow. They asked one of the ostlers to ride into the village and report the death, the ostler did so and said he thought it would be a pauper's funeral. Mr Grimshaw, the Parish clerk, said, 'We will have to fetch the body on a sledge as I don't think a horse and cart would be able to get through.' The man agreed with him and they decided that Mr Grimshaw would be along in the morning to make all arrangements. The ostler made his way back to the George and relayed the news that the clerk would come in the morning with the undertaker to fetch the body.

The next day they did, indeed, arrive with a horse and sledge. Meg invited them into the parlour as Mr Grimshaw told her he would need details of the tragedy. He asked Meg if she knew the lady's name and Meg replied unfortunately she did not as the lady was dead when she arrived and she had no identification on her. She explained that she was on top of the coach with the baby wrapped inside her cloak and no identification on either of them. They discussed when they thought the road might be open again and both thought it might be passable in a couple of days.

Mr Grimshaw went to the corn store and asked for some assistance to move Emma onto the sledge. He asked the coachman if he had any further information but all the coachman could tell him was where he had picked Emma up. They searched Emma's cloak pockets to see if there was anything there that might identify them and found a receipt from the workhouse. The clerk said, 'I will give this piece of paper to Meg Jolly as she will want to know that the baby's name is Elizabeth.' Dusk fell quickly at that time of year and Mr Grimshaw said he must return before night came.

He went back up to the inn to speak to Meg and Winton and to tell them he had found no document of identification but had found the receipt from the workhouse. He told them it would be a pauper's funeral but Meg was not happy about this and she said she thought other arrangements could perhaps be made. She went into the bar and told the travellers there of Mr Grimshaw's announcement and asked whether they would be prepared to contribute to a collection so the lady would not have a pauper's funeral.

One of the gentlemen said he would contribute a guinea and all the rest of the passengers said they would contribute. Meg collected just under two guineas and took the money to Mr Grimshaw who said that would be sufficient to bury the lady in the churchyard in a reasonable plot. He asked what they wanted put on the headstone, they thought for a minute and the gentleman who gave the guinea said, 'As we don't know her name, I think it should just say *Not forgotten; always remembered*.' Everybody agreed with this wording as none of them would forget the tragedy of that journey.

Mr Grimshaw then told Meg more about the receipt from the workhouse and the fact that the baby's name was Elizabeth. He asked her what the position was with the baby and Meg replied that she thought it would be better if they kept her there. Mr Grimshaw thought that was a good idea, much better than taking her back to the workhouse. Therefore, it was arranged that Meg would keep Elizabeth and bring her up, so a sad story would have a happy ending. Mr Grimshaw then returned to the village to see to the burial.

The coachman told all the passengers he was intending to make a start in the morning and they could get on their way as the snow has started to melt and the road was passable. Early next morning the coach set off on its onward journey, the horses were hitched to the coach and the passengers climbed aboard; there was not much jollity as the journey had been a sad and long one.

Meg and Winton stood on the steps and watched as the coach disappeared down the road.

★ ★ ★

At Cheswardine, Miss Charlotte and Daniel had many problems to sort out: Roderick had died and the burial was the first priority; Emma was missing; Jane had gone but the baby was also missing. The situation was very difficult but Miss Charlotte took charge and informed the Sheriff and his assistant that the baby and Emma were missing. She knew that Jane had taken a lot of the silver and she wanted a warrant for her arrest. The Sheriff sent a message to say he would come the following morning.

The Sheriff arrived with his Deputy as promised and they were shown into the library. Miss Charlotte, in her competent way, had made a full list of all the items that Jane had taken, which she presented to the Sheriff. He took the list and asked Miss Charlotte if she had she any idea where Jane might have gone with the baby but she replied, 'No, I have no idea where she is but she has taken the trinkets for payment and the baby out of spite.'

The Sheriff asked her about Emma, whom they believed was missing as well and Miss Charlotte answered, 'Yes, Emma, the housekeeper, is missing, too. At the moment, this is not a very happy household.'

The Sheriff noted all Miss Charlotte had told him then he said it was a difficult situation, as they had just had the biggest snowstorm for many years and most of the roads were impassable, people were licking their wounds and clearing up. He told her that would not stand in his way and he would pursue the matter and try to find the baby and look for Jane. He said to her, 'I will do everything I can but you must appreciate the storm has caused a lot of damage and so it will take longer to conclude the matter.'

Miss Charlotte told him she understood perfectly but they would appreciate it if he could start to make some investigations into the matter as they had had a lot of sorrow in the family and would like the baby returned. The Sheriff told her he understood and would do everything possible.

Miss Charlotte arranged for Roderick's funeral to take place, it had been difficult as the ground was frozen so it had been delayed, but the task needed to be done. She sent word to Quaker Allen of the date of the funeral and that he would be very welcome to come, particularly as they had already agreed that Roderick was to be buried alongside Sarah, side by side with his permission.

Miss Charlotte carried on with the arrangements for the funeral. She arranged with the estate workers to have Roderick's body put on a dray to take him to the Quaker plot in the cemetery. The gravediggers told Miss Charlotte the ground was too hard but the solution would be to light a fire on the spot and then it would make it easier to dig. They piled logs and kindling on the plot and then lit the fire. It seemed everything was going wrong and nothing right and Miss Charlotte felt overwhelmed by it all. There had been so much happiness but now it seemed to have all disappeared and they were all surrounded by sorrow.

On the day of Roderick's funeral, his father, Miss Charlotte and Daniel arrived at Cheswardine. Roderick's body was put on the dray, there were no flowers as it was midwinter and everything was still covered in snow, so Miss Charlotte had asked Abel to cut some holly and ivy to place on the coffin. Two beautiful shire horses pulled the dray, behind the dray the coach drew up. Miss Charlotte, Daniel and his father boarded the coach and another coach for the servants from the house followed. Behind them, all the workers from the estate walked in a solemn procession.

Joining them at the crossroads, the Quakers came to pay their respects. Quaker Allen, his wife and daughters joined the procession. They all walked behind the funeral cortège as it made its way to the cemetery. Not a lot of people attended as the weather was so inclement and Roderick had not gathered many friends who wished to say goodbye.

The procession wound its way through the churchyard to the church where the vicar gave a short sermon. He told the congregation they were all there to say goodbye to Roderick and he hoped he would be reunited with Sarah and they would be together for eternity. A hymn was sung, prayers said, and the congregation shuffled out of the church to the graveyard. Some of the estate workers carried the coffin to the grave. As the coffin was lowered into the ground, each of the family threw some soil onto the coffin as the vicar said a last prayer. The family moved away from the grave and the gravediggers started filling the grave in.

Quaker Allen came over to Miss Charlotte, grasped her hand and said, 'They are laid together now. We can do no more. I would like to thank you for your kindness to my daughter and I wish you all good fortune in the future.' He set off with his wife and daughters, feeling he had more than enough sorrow to bear and wanted to leave it all behind and return to his home.

Miss Charlotte told Daniel and his father they would make their way to Cheswardine as there was business there that needed to be discussed. They boarded the coach and made their way back to Cheswardine, all keeping their thoughts to themselves and making the journey in silence. Half an hour later they arrived back at the house where they saw smoke coming from the chimneys and knew they would be able to sit in warmth and comfort. Abel was already back there to greet them; he opened the coach door and helped Miss Charlotte alight. She squeezed his hand as he did so and said, 'Thank you, Abel, for everything,' then entered the house.

They all went into the library where a fire had been lit. It looked very cosy and was some comfort as they sat down to discuss the future of Cheswardine. Miss Charlotte rang the bell and asked the maid to fetch a tray of tea as they had a lot of business to discuss.

They sat around the fire and Miss Charlotte began, 'There is a problem to solve and I think now is the time to do this.' Daniel sat there and thought to himself that you never know what life is going to throw at you until it comes. His mother said to him that there were two options as far as she could see: either to sell Cheswardine or they could run it as a small estate. She asked Daniel if he would be interested in running the estate and dividing his time between that and the foundry. He replied that if it was his mother's wish, he would do so. Miss Charlotte was very pleased, she did not want to sell Cheswardine as it had been in the family for such a long time. There was some happiness in the house but it had to be sought, she told them there had been so much unhappiness there must be some happiness to come. They were all agreed that Daniel would run the estate; he would spend half of his time at the foundry and the other half at the estate.

Miss Charlotte then said, 'There is another situation we have to resolve, our granddaughter, Elizabeth, is missing and we have no idea where she is. Emma is also missing and we don't know where she is either. This could not have happened at a worse time as the country is in a frozen state and it is so difficult to get about. I have notified the Sheriff but will ask him if he could put some more men on the case to find them both.'

Daniel agreed with the plan, Elizabeth's home was Cheswardine and that is where she should be.

Miss Charlotte thought putting up a reward of five guineas for any information of the baby, Elizabeth Torduff, might be a good idea to see if that would help. The next day, she met with the Sheriff and told him she would pay a reward of five guineas for any information. The Sheriff thought this was a good idea as a reward always loosened people's lips. Therefore, they agreed to post the notice seeking Elizabeth Torduff with details of the reward.

Days turned into weeks, which turned into months, and there was still no sign of where Elizabeth and Emma had gone. Miss Charlotte did not believe they could have vanished and once again, she sent for the Sheriff. He came and told Miss Charlotte extensive enquiries had been made and Jane, who had taken the silver trinkets, could not be traced either. The last sighting of Emma and the baby had been of her walking along the Great North Road. They knew the baby had been taken to the workhouse to be fed but then left there, and then someone, that they assumed to be Emma, had taken her out after paying one guinea. Emma must have then set off walking along the Great North Road and nobody had seen her or the baby since that night.

I cannot believe nobody has seen them and that they have disappeared without trace,' said Miss Charlotte.

The Sheriff replied, 'This happens sometimes and one day we will have a satisfactory answer.'

Miss Charlotte looked at the Sheriff, 'You have not brought me any satisfactory answers and I want my granddaughter back so we will have to resolve this puzzle ourselves.' The Sheriff knew she would never be satisfied until the mystery was solved and her granddaughter had been returned to Cheswardine.

Abel came into the library where Miss Charlotte, Daniel and his father, the gunmaker Torduff, were sitting and said he would like a word with them. He had a problem with Miss Sarah's pony, Jess and with Bluebell, Roderick's horse. They had both become very restless as they were missing their owners, especially Bluebell as she had been very attached to Miss Sarah as she visited her every day and took her treats. Charlotte replied, 'Horses do become very attached to their masters and mistresses, they go on smell. I suggest, Abel, you take Jess out of the stable and give the stable a thorough cleaning, walls, harnesses and anything Miss Sarah might have touched. I think you will have to burn all the rugs, as you will not be able to remove the smell. Then I should put both of them in adjoining stalls so they will be company for each other. It will take a week or two for them to acclimatise to their new surroundings and each other's company.'

Abel thought Miss Charlotte was drawing on many years of experience as she had been born in the country and raised at Cheswardine, she was tapping into the knowledge she had learnt over those years and Abel knew she was right.

Daniel asked his mother if he could take over Bluebell, he would need a good horse as he would be riding between Chimneys and Cheswardine. She told him she had no misgivings and thought it was a good idea. Miss Charlotte looked at Daniel and Abel and told them she thought they should all start to think about the future and must stop living in the past. She thought it would be more rewarding as they could not change the past, that is already sealed but the future is untouched. Abel and Daniel agreed with her.

She then said she thought they must clear Roderick's and Sarah's bedroom and remove all clothes and personal belongings, she wanted Roderick's clothes burnt as he would not like anyone to wear any of his clothes and the same would go for Sarah's clothes. Miss Charlotte called for Polly and they went up to the main bedroom and started to empty all the drawers and wardrobes, wrapping things in large bundles. She turned to Polly and asked her where Emma's room was and Polly told her it was at the top of the house. Miss Charlotte told Polly she would go up there and start to clear Emma's things too.

She did the same in Emma's room, collected all the clothes, put them in a bundle, and took them down. She told Polly she wanted her to take them into the paddock and light a fire to burn them all. Polly asked her if she intended to burn everything, Miss Charlotte told her that, yes, everything was to be burnt, and then they could all make a fresh start and see if they could bring some good luck into the house, there had been enough bad luck. Polly agreed with her, called Abel to give them some assistance and they took all the clothes into the paddock. Abel fetched kindling and lit the fire; once it had taken hold, they placed the clothes on the flames. Smoke billowed upwards and Miss Charlotte, Polly, and Abel knew that was the beginning of a new start.

In spite of their hope for some good luck, days turned into weeks, weeks into months and months into years but there was no sign of Elizabeth. Everyone still lived in hope that one day she would return but there was never any sign of her, so life carried on.

CHAPTER 9

The George Inn

At the George Inn, Winton and Meg had carried on with their lives. Elizabeth had been there for seven years and she had blossomed into a very pretty child, the apple of Meg's eye.

At the inn everyone had their chores to do but the tack was never put away as it was a full-time job. The first coaches arrived at the inn at six o'clock in the morning and the last one arrived at midnight, the horses had to be fed and groomed and the coaches cleaned so it was a very busy life.

Elizabeth often helped Meg in the kitchen, Meg was an excellent cook and the George had a good reputation for its food. Elizabeth liked being in the kitchen and Meg enjoyed her company; it was a good combination and worked well. It was a hard life but the inn was a happy place.

It was Winton's name over the door as the landlord but it was Meg who ran the inn. They opened at five in the morning and people would come in for rum and coffee before going on their way to work at the local foundries. The working day was six to six and one of the Elizabeth's jobs was to serve the foundry men their rum and coffee before they started their toil. She used to light the fire so the inn was warm before the men arrived. Another of Elizabeth's tasks was to knock all the dents out of the pewter mugs. This was done by putting them on a last and knocking them with a mallet to remove the dents. It was a busy life in the inn and one of the most time-consuming jobs was to keep all the food tables fully supplied. Meg was kept busy cooking and producing hot food for the weary travellers.

One of Elizabeth's outside jobs, which she enjoyed, was to feed the pigs all the waste from the kitchen. When she fetched the food bucket from the kitchen, the pigs would know she was coming to feed them and would run over to her, snuffling and grunting, pleased to see her. Everyone in the inn could hear the pigs and knew it was their breakfast time. Elizabeth would lean over and scratch the pigs' backs and talk to them, Meg had told her not to give them names as she did not want her to become attached to them as they would eventually go for slaughter. This did not stop Elizabeth from liking them and the pigs used to run up to the wall when they saw Elizabeth, as they knew she would scratch their backs. Another of Elizabeth's jobs was to fetch the milk from the dairy; they had a dairymaid at the inn who looked after the cows. Being on the Great North Road and so busy, the inn always needed a good supply of milk for the kitchen. There were two milk cows that the dairymaid looked after; she also made all the butter and cheese.

The inn had its own laundry and two laundry maids came in on Mondays, Tuesdays and Wednesdays. They used pearl ash, soda and hard soap to wash all the linen. A lot of clean linen was needed as all the beds were changed after each traveller. The linen was washed and dried in the laundry and then put in linen presses to keep it fresh.

The inn also had its own brewery; this was an essential part of their trade as each inn brewed its own ale for the travellers. The inn brewed every week; it was a major operation. mixing the barley, the malted barley, the water and the yeast. Winton was the brewer and he took great pride in producing good ale for all the travelling customers. The excise man would come every week and dip the barrels; the excise duty was two shillings a barrel for the strong beer, one shilling for the weaker beer. This had to be paid by law, the revenue man could arrive at any time, Monday to Saturday. Winton decided he would brew on a Sunday as he thought he would not have to pay revenue for the beer he brewed on a Sunday. He said, 'Six days for King George and Sunday for Winton Jolly,' which he thought was very fair!

Meg thought it was time Elizabeth had some form of education and should go to school. Their other children went to school and she thought Elizabeth should join them. She was a forward-looking woman and believed all women should be educated as well as men. She told Elizabeth she was going to the penny school with the other children; she would have to leave at half-past seven in the morning to arrive at the school at half-past eight. Meg told Elizabeth she would need to learn how to ride the pony as that is how she would travel to school. Meg's eldest son, Noah, would teach her how to ride. Meg told Elizabeth the best pony to ride would be one of the Welsh Cobs as they were sure-footed animals, good to ride and intelligent. Meg said, 'Noah will teach you well and, when it is time to go to school, you will feel very confident.'

Meg also told Elizabeth she would need some new clothes for school so Mr Scrivens the tailor would come and measure her for some riding clothes, some dresses and a new cloak, as the early mornings could be very cold and she wanted to be sure she arrived at school warm and dry.

Elizabeth started her riding lessons with Noah in the paddock. She took to riding like a duck to water. The pony she was riding was called Sambo, he was quite old but sure footed and Noah told her he would take his time and not run away with her. It was like a gift from God to Elizabeth, she took to the pony as if it was second nature. Sambo had taken to Elizabeth too, especially as she took him a carrot every morning and he came to rely on her appearance at the same time each day. He would wait by the fence for Elizabeth to bring him his carrot, this created a bond between them, a little bit of love on both sides and that is what makes the world go round.

Mr Scrivens, the tailor, arrived one day and Elizabeth went in to be measured. Meg told him she wanted him to make a good cloak with a double lining, so the wet and snow would not go through. Meg thought a silk lining would be nice and asked if he had some samples so they could choose there and then. Elizabeth looked at the samples and together they chose a dark coloured woollen cloth and a dark blue silk for the lining. A large hood was requested with blue ribbon around it and large inner pockets in the cloak. She was also measured for some woollen dresses to wear to school. He was a capable tailor and Meg had used his services many times and had always been satisfied with his work. The Jollys were not landed gentry but trade: they worked hard for their money, they were careful but not mean, so Elizabeth had the best they could afford.

The day arrived for Elizabeth to go to school; Sambo was saddled and ready. Meg had made lunch for all five of them and put it in the saddlebags; also in the saddlebags was some corn for Sambo and the other ponies. The corn was divided into three eating bags and at lunchtime each pony was given a bag round his head and that is how he ate his lunch. The Jollys were very horse orientated, they had dealt with horses and ponies all of their lives. At half past seven in the morning, Elizabeth came down and mounted Sambo. There were two other ponies: Meg's other children rode two on each, Annabel rode one with Noah and Samuel and Lyndon rode together on the other. Noah led the way on the first pony, Elizabeth came second and Samuel last.

It was a lovely morning, the sun was shining, the sky was blue and the trees were in full leaf. They had seven and a half miles to go to the school. As they passed a bad bend with a large oak, all the ponies suddenly started to gallop with no orders from their riders. As they passed the oak, Elizabeth noticed there was a gibbet hanging there. She rode to Noah's side and asked why the ponies had galloped past the tree. Noah told her that was the hanging tree where all the highwaymen were hanged and they always passed it at least at a trot. 'We always feel it is a sad place to pass, the horses are used to it and as they approach the hanging tree they gallop faster and once passed, they slow down again.'

As they approached the school, they could hear the school bell ringing. They rode into the schoolyard, dismounted and put the ponies in their shelter; then took their saddles off and hung them up on a saddle stand. There were other ponies in the shelter as it was a large, spread out community and using ponies was the only way to reach the school.

The school was a church school, financed by the local gentry and the local farmers. They believed in education for the young, as later in life everyone would reap the benefits. It was one of the first church schools built. It was a large stone building with a house attached for the master, which was the custom. The pupils were mostly from farming stock, as it was a farming community. There was one large classroom with a big chimney in the centre and a large grate for a log fire, as it got very cold in the winter.

The head of the school was Mr Grace. He was a tall man with thinning hair and a bony face; he had a gentle voice, which was a pleasure to listen to. There were two rows of desks, boys on one side and girls on the other. A large blackboard stood at the end of the room, near to the fire. Each desk had two slates with chalk for writing on them. Mr Grace stood at the head of the class as the pupils filed in. He said good morning to everyone and they all replied, 'Good morning, Sir.'

He walked down the aisle between the desks looking at each pupil, until he arrived at the desk where Elizabeth was sitting. He stopped and enquired what her name was.

She replied, 'It's Elizabeth, Sir.'

He said, 'Welcome to our small community, we hope you will be happy here. You are here to acquire knowledge so don't waste a minute, learning will equip you for the rest of your life.'

He then went to the head of the class and read out all the names and as he did so the children replied and he ticked them off in the register. It was a small class of fifteen pupils, which was average for the size of the community although it was a large area.

The day went on and she enjoyed the lessons as it was something new and she could join in. The classroom was warm, the teacher was pleasant, and the atmosphere was conducive to learning. Mr Grace was a good teacher; he had a lot of knowledge and was happy to pass it on to his pupils. The school atmosphere was pleasant, everyone seemed very friendly, and Elizabeth felt very happy. Mr Grace noticed Elizabeth was an intelligent child and thought she would go far in life so he paid particular attention to her. Her handwriting was clear and tidy and she had a good understanding of the topic taught, he thought she had all the ingredients in life to make a success of her education.

Time went on and the bell went for dinnertime. Elizabeth went out to look at the ponies and to give them some corn. She went to the shelter and Sambo brightened up as soon as he saw her. Animals decide who they like, he liked Elizabeth, and the feeling was mutual. She put her hands round his neck, gave him a kiss, and told him he was a good boy. Then she put his feedbag on so he could munch his corn. She waited until he had finished, then went to the well, and fetched him some water. Elizabeth had never been taught to do these things but they seemed to come naturally. She then fetched her own lunch, and went and sat in the schoolyard with the other pupils. It was a lovely day and she enjoyed her lunch, she learnt the other pupils' names and chatted to them. She learnt they were mostly from good families and had good manners and included her in their conversations. The lunch hour passed very quickly, the bell rang and lunchtime was finished.

They all filed back into the classroom, boys one side, and girls on the other. Mr Grace stood at the head of the class and they settled down for an afternoon of study. When the bell rang at half past three, Mr Grace came over to Elizabeth and asked, 'Have you enjoyed your first day, Elizabeth?'

She replied, 'Very much, Sir. It has been a very pleasant day.' Mr Grace smiled at her and was pleased with the compliment.

The children filed out of school and went to the shelter to saddle the ponies. Samuel helped Elizabeth saddle Sambo and, once all the ponies were saddled, they mounted them and went on their way, back to the George Inn. Once again, as they were trotting past the hanging tree, the ponies galloped as fast as they could to pass the tree.

When they arrived at the George, Meg came out and asked them if they had all had a good day and they all said they had. She went to Elizabeth and asked, 'How was your first day at school?'

Elizabeth hugged her, 'Thank you for sending me to school and for my lovely cloak and Sambo and I had a lovely day at school.' Meg told her she did not need to thank her as she had brought a lot of happiness to the George and to them. They all went into the inn and, like children everywhere, they were hungry so Meg set out some food and, as she watched them tucking in, felt she was very much blessed with them all. Meg said to the children that there would be a month at school and then they would break up, so they could help with the harvest and the shearing of the sheep. This was how it was in the country: they had long breaks in the summer and the autumn to get ready for winter.

Next morning the children were ready for school, the ponies were fetched and the children mounted them and rode off. They passed the hanging tree and the ponies again broke into a gallop to pass as quickly as possible. They arrived at school on time, the register was taken and everyone was present. The little girl sitting next to Elizabeth asked her what her name was, Elizabeth told her and then the girl wanted to know where she lived so Elizabeth told her she lived at The George. She asked the girl her name. 'My name is Annabelle and I live at Hough Manor with my father but I will not be coming to school again as Father is hiring a governess so I can be taught at home.'

'You're having a governess, but won't you miss coming to school?' asked Elizabeth.

'Yes,' said Annabelle, 'But my father thinks I would concentrate more on lessons in my own home. I shall miss coming to school and I am wondering what the new governess will be like. Father said she is a nice lady and it would be an advantage to have a good education, because a good education prepares you for all life's ups and downs.'

Elizabeth and Annabelle spent the whole day together and were soon firm friends. As the afternoon bell rang, Elizabeth said to Annabelle, 'I expect I'll never see you again. I enjoyed your company and I wish you all good fortune and happiness with your new governess.' She leant forward and kissed Annabelle goodbye and Annabelle kissed Elizabeth in return and sadly said goodbye.

The children went to collect their ponies, it was a wet, miserable day and both children and ponies knew it was going to be a wet, miserable ride home. Elizabeth pulled her hood over her head and urged Sambo onwards. They all arrived in the yard at The George and the ostlers came out to take care of the ponies.

Elizabeth and the others went into the inn, Meg enquired after their day and told them to sit in the kitchen and she would bring them some hot food. They all sat round the table looking forward to the meal, as Meg was a very good cook. Meg knew it was better to feed the children as soon as they arrived home as they were always hungry and the coaches did not start arriving until later on and, once they did, the work was non-stop.

The next morning was bright and dry and, as they rode their ponies to school, Elizabeth thought she would miss Annabelle. The day passed, new lessons were learnt and it was soon time to go home. The journey home was uneventful except for the ponies galloping past the hanging tree as usual. When they arrived home, the ostler again took the ponies, unsaddled them, rubbed them down and fed them and soon they were in their nice comfortable stable.

Meg was waiting at the door, 'I want a word with you, Elizabeth. I have had a visitor today from Jonathon Grantham from Hough Manor. He told me you sat next to his daughter Annabelle at school and you had become friends. He wanted to know if, with my permission, you would like to take lessons with Annabelle and the governess at Hough Manor. He said he would send a horse and trap for you in the morning and the same to bring you back in the evening.'

Elizabeth was taken aback but said, 'Yes please, I would like that very much because Annabelle and I really got on very well. I did not expect to see her again, but it seems we are going to meet again and become better friends.' Meg told Elizabeth she would send a message to Jonathon Grantham to say they had agreed with the arrangements.

Meg was up early the next day and told Elizabeth to put her best dress and bonnet on and to use her best cloak. She said, 'It will make a good impression and in life you only get one chance when you first meet someone so the first impression is very important.'

In due course the pony and trap arrived in the inn yard and Meg went out to greet him. The driver said, 'Good morning, Madam. My name is Mr Jeremy,' and Meg replied, 'Good morning to you, please take good care of Miss Elizabeth.'

Mr Jeremy said that of course he would and would return her safely at the end of the day. He helped Elizabeth into the trap and made sure she had a blanket over her legs. Meg thought how smart he looked in his full livery with silver buttons and a top hat; she stood and watched them drive away, a new life starting for Elizabeth.

Elizabeth said, 'Please Sir, how should I address you?' and he replied, 'You should call me Mr Jeremy and I will call you Miss Elizabeth.' He told her that, to make the journey more enjoyable, they would look out for birds on the way and see how many they could name and see how many animals crossed their path. As they went along the road, Mr Jeremy pointed out many birds and so Elizabeth's education had started. Jeremy had lived in the country for a long time and had worked for the family for many years. He was a trusted servant and would be looking after Elizabeth, fetching her and then returning her at the end of the day. The journey passed with plenty of sightings of different birds and animals as they drove through the wooded countryside, which made it very interesting.

When they arrived at the Manor, they drove down the drive and Elizabeth could see Annabelle and her father – Jonathon Grantham – waiting for her. The trap drew up outside the Manor and Jonathon Grantham stepped forward to help Elizabeth step down from the trap.

Elizabeth said, 'Good morning, Sir.'

Jonathon looked at her and smiled, 'You must call me Mr Jonathon.'

Elizabeth replied, 'Thank you, Sir, Mr Jonathon,' and they all laughed.

'You are a guest of Hough Manor, a guest of Annabelle and my guest.'

'Thank you,' Elizabeth replied.

Jonathon Grantham came from a good family, landed gentry who had farmed the land for a thousand years so he did not need to impress anyone. He took Elizabeth's hand, 'If you would like to follow me, I will introduce you to the housekeeper, Mrs Morris,' and they walked through the hall. It was an old Elizabethan manor with carved oak panelling and, at the end of the hall, stood Mrs Morris. She smiled at Elizabeth, 'Welcome to Hough Manor. I believe your name is Miss Elizabeth.'

Mrs Morris told Elizabeth she would show her around the Manor, she would soon know her way about and would feel more comfortable. Elizabeth already felt comfortable with Mrs Morris and the house felt warm and welcoming. Mrs Morris took her to the kitchens and showed her around; she then took her to the library, sitting room, dining room and told Elizabeth that lessons with the Governess were to take place in the old nursery on the top floor.

After the tour, they went up to the nursery where there were two desks and two chairs, one ready for each of them. Elizabeth felt quite at home and, chatting with Annabelle, Annabelle asked if she liked horses. Elizabeth replied, 'Yes, very much,' and Annabelle suggested they went down to the stables and met Snowball, who was her pony. They went downstairs and out of the side door to the stables, in the end stable was a pure white Welsh Cob. Elizabeth asked Annabelle if that was her pony and Annabelle replied, 'Yes, she is and I ride her whenever I can.'

As they walked through the stables they came to a loose box where there was a large hunter in residence; his name on the door was 'Rainbow'. Annabelle explained he was her mother's horse and she had lost her life whilst out hunting as Rainbow could not take a fence and her mother had fallen and was killed.

Nobody could do anything with Rainbow, as her mother had always looked after him and none of the grooms could manage him so he was going to the knacker's yard. He had to be fed over the stable door as he was so difficult, he didn't like men and all the grooms were frightened of him. As they spoke, a groom approached with a fork full of hay and, as soon as Rainbow saw him, he turned round in his stable and started kicking the door.

'Don't go near him, he will harm you if you do,' said the groom. But Elizabeth looked at Rainbow and the horse was looking at her, she put her hand out to him and he came up to the door. Annabelle could not believe her eyes, it was as if they were instant friends. Sometimes in the animal kingdom this happens, animals and humans look at one another and a bond is formed. Elizabeth put her hand over the stable door and rubbed

Rainbow's nose, he snickered in reply; she thought she could make friends with Rainbow.

As they walked on through the stables, Elizabeth asked Annabelle if her father would agree for her to go and see Rainbow each day. Annabelle said she thought he would but her father was planning to give him to the knackerman when he came on his monthly visit, as he couldn't be ridden or groomed.

When they got back to the house and made their way to the nursery, the governess, Miss Jones, was waiting for them. She went straight to Annabelle and said, 'Good morning, Miss Annabelle and is this your new friend?'

Annabelle introduced Elizabeth and Miss Jones shook hands with Elizabeth and said, 'Welcome to Hough Manor. I hope you are going to enjoy our lessons. On nice days we can sit in the garden and have our lessons outside and on bad days we will sit in the nursery.' Elizabeth thought Miss Jones was a nice gentle lady and she would enjoy being taught by her and would learn a lot.

They sat down and lessons began. Miss Jones told them she would start with lessons of etiquette as they would need to know how to dine, how to greet people, how to behave in public as befitted two young ladies and that this was just as important as reading, writing and arithmetic.

Miss Jones told the girls that good manners open many doors and never go out of fashion, but bad manners are always remembered. The two girls looked at each other and smiled, their day had begun. Miss Jones was a good teacher and the morning went very quickly. She told the girls to go to the kitchen for their lunch and she would see them afterwards. They would work until half past three and then Mr Jeremy would take Miss Elizabeth home.

The girls went down to the kitchen where the cook told them their lunch was ready. Elizabeth asked the cook, 'Would it be in order if I asked for an apple to take out to Rainbow?'

The cook smiled, 'That would be perfectly in order, now come and eat your lunch.' The girls sat at the table, enjoying their lunch, and chatted as if they had known each other for a very long time. The cook smiled to herself, pleased that Miss Annabelle finally had a friend.

Elizabeth asked Annabelle if she would like to go out to the stable with her as she wanted to give Rainbow a present and Annabelle told her she would like very much to come. After lunch, the two girls left the kitchen through the back door, out to the stables. As they walked in, there was Rainbow with his head over the stable door, watching them as they walked towards him. His ears went straight up, he made a snickering noise, and Elizabeth knew they were going to be friends. She walked up to the stable door and gave him the apple, which he took very gently; he munched away as if it was his birthday. 'I think he is going to like you very much,' said Annabelle, 'You are the only one he has taken to on the estate.'

They returned to the nursery and continued their lessons until half past three when Mr Jeremy was waiting at the door for Elizabeth. He helped her into the trap and, as they set off for the George, he asked if she had enjoyed her lessons. She replied, 'I have enjoyed the lessons and my day very much and look forward to coming back every day.'

'Then count your blessings,' Jeremy said.

As they rode along, they both enjoyed the countryside. Elizabeth asked many questions about the birds she saw and the plants. Mr Jeremy was a mine of information and she enjoyed the journey very much.

As they drew into the yard at The George, Jeremy looked at Elizabeth, 'I am pleased you enjoyed your day at Hough Manor and I hope you enjoy your time there,' then he helped Miss Elizabeth alight. She thanked him and he said he would see her in the morning.

Meg was waiting in the doorway and Elizabeth ran to greet her. Meg hugged her, 'I have missed you so much and was wondering how your day had gone.'

'It was wonderful, I have a lovely friend in Annabelle and I have also made another friend, a horse called Rainbow.' Elizabeth told Meg all about her day and how she had enjoyed herself and was looking forward to going back in the morning.

Life fell into a routine, Jeremy picked Elizabeth up each day and took her to the Manor. As time went by, the lessons became more interesting and the more Elizabeth learnt, the more she wanted to know. Each day, after lunch, the cook gave Elizabeth an apple and both girls went out to see Rainbow. The horse knew what time the girls would go to see him and he waited at his stable door. A rapport gradually built between Elizabeth and Rainbow and he would let her stroke him; each day they became better friends. He would greet Elizabeth with a snicker and would let her put her arms around his neck.

One day Elizabeth decided when she went to visit Rainbow she would go when none of the grooms was around and she would go into Rainbow's stall. She undid the door and went into the stall, Rainbow made a funny noise and looked at her, she went up close to him and he nuzzled her and whinnied with delight. This was the first time anyone on the estate had been able to approach Rainbow; it was almost as if Elizabeth had broken down some invisible barrier, this large hunter and this young girl had developed an understanding, a bond no-one else had managed to forge since his mistress had died.

Elizabeth thought it was time for Rainbow to have a walk and to come out of his stable so she fetched a lead rein and attached it to his halter. She walked him along the passageway into the stable yard; Rainbow snickered with pleasure and nuzzled Elizabeth's hand as she walked him around the yard. As they walked, the grooms came to see where the clatter of hooves was coming from. They were amazed to see Elizabeth with Rainbow and were all rendered speechless until one of them thought they should let the master know. One of the grooms went off to fetch him and the others watched in astonishment at the rapport Elizabeth had with the large hunter who was supposed to be uncontrollable, a nasty, vicious animal.

Mr Jonathon arrived already dressed for riding and he too looked on in amazement, 'If I had not seen it myself I would not have believed it was possible; Rainbow on a lead rein walking around the stable yard. A fortnight ago none of us would dare go near him. We must put this down to the determination of a little girl to put some happiness in a horse's life.'

Elizabeth walked him around the yard once more and decided it was time to take him back to his stall; he went into his stall with no problems. His ears pricked up as Elizabeth fetched his hay down and put it into his feed basket, they both looked at each other and a friendship was sealed.

As Elizabeth shut the stable door and walked up the passageway, Mr Jonathon was waiting for her.

'If I had not seen that with my own eyes I would not have believed it was possible. That was my wife's horse and she raised him from young to the hunter he is today but nobody could handle him other than my wife. When she died in the hunting accident he was impossible to control; he was destined to go to the knacker's yard but it seems there is a glimmer of hope now.'

Elizabeth looked at him, 'You will not send him to the knacker's yard now, will you, Mr Jonathon?'

He looked at Elizabeth and said, 'No, I won't. Let's share this piece of happiness. We will keep Rainbow but you now have a task for life, you will have to look after him.'

'I will gladly look after him, Mr Jonathon,' Elizabeth replied.

Jonathon turned around and walked back up the stable yard, still in shock at the turn of events. He was still grieving after the death of his wife in the hunting accident but, like most men, he kept the sorrow to himself and did not want to share it with anybody. Sorrow takes a long time to heal and, in Mr Jonathon's case, it was taking a particularly long time to heal.

But life went on, months and then years passed with the girls enjoying their lessons and their life on the estate until, one year, when it came to the time for the hunt ball, which was always held at Hough Manor.

CHAPTER 10

Hough Manor

Three weeks before the ball, there was a meeting of the Hunt, this happened every Tuesday in the hunting season. Jonathon was Master of the Hunt, as his father and grandfather had been before him. The hounds were kept at Hough Manor, in an area away from the stables and were looked after by a head huntsman and his assistant.

All the neighbours attended the meet on the Tuesday, they gathered outside the front door and the footman came out carrying a tray with stirrup cups, which he handed round to the riders. The maids came out with refreshments, it was traditional in that area that black pudding and savoury pies were offered to the riders. There were thirty people all dressed in their hunting clothes, the hunting pink striking a memorable picture. The chief huntsman blew his horn, the dogs led the way and the riders followed down the lane, a typical English scene.

Annabelle and Elizabeth watched the scene from one of the downstairs rooms. They marvelled at the spectacle, the colours of the clothes, the hounds milling about, the horses snorting and ready for the off. The ladies rode side saddle and looked very elegant. They watched as they all galloped down the lane ready for a day's hunting.

The girls then returned to the schoolroom but Miss Jones was not well so there would not be any formal lessons. They decided they would explore the house and, as they came to the main floor, Annabelle suggested they go into her mother's bedroom. They went into the room where they found all the furniture covered with dustsheets. Annabelle told Elizabeth her father no longer came into this room, as it was too painful for him.

Annabelle went to the wardrobe and opened the door, 'These are Mama's dresses; nobody ever wears them now.' She pulled one of the dresses down and said she was going to try it on, as she liked it very much. She stood looking at herself in the mirror but then the door opened and Mr Jonathon stood in the doorway. The expression on his face was one of horror as the likeness between Annabelle and her mother was striking.

'Take that dress off at once and never come into this room again, go back to the nursery and look at your books.' The girls left feeling very chastened and returned to the nursery.

Jonathon rang the bell and a footman arrived, he told the footman he wanted everything in the room removed to the paddock and burnt. The footman said,' Everything, Sir? All the furniture as well?'

'Yes,' replied Jonathon, 'Everything.' The footman called for assistance and all the clothes and furniture were removed and taken to the paddock. Jonathon followed them out to the paddock where the footmen had set fire to all the furniture and clothes. He stood and watched everything burning and thought to himself, that is the end of that, I think I should have a new beginning. Jonathon thought the time had come to move on as he could not continue to live in the past and he could not alter the terrible tragedy that had occurred. He thought life must go on and now was time for change.

He went back to the house and up to the nursery where the girls were reading their books; he looked at them and sat on one of the desks. He said to Annabelle, 'Would you like Elizabeth to come and live here with you, study with you and be a friend? She can have the bedroom next to yours and it will be company for you both.'

Annabelle flung her arms around her father, 'Oh yes, I would love that very much, if Elizabeth's parents will agree.'

Jonathon looked at Elizabeth, 'Would you like to come and live at Hough Manor? We can try to see how it would work out, I think it would do both of you some good to have each other's company, apart from your lessons together.'

Elizabeth looked at him, 'Yes sir, I would very much like that, as long as my parents are happy with the plan and I can visit them.'

Jonathon told them he would visit Elizabeth's parents and ask their permission for the move. Jonathon left the girls talking excitedly and went downstairs. He rang the bell and asked the footman to send the housekeeper to him. Mrs Morris came and Jonathon said, 'Mrs Morris, Miss Elizabeth will probably be coming to stay at Hough Manor and I think the bedroom next to Miss Annabelle's would be perfect for her.'

'Yes Sir, I think that is a very good idea. Miss Elizabeth is a very nice young lady and I think it is a good idea for Miss Annabelle to have some company. This is a big house and I think Miss Annabelle must be lonely sometimes. I will see to the bedroom straight away.'

'Mrs Morris, please will you ask one of the grooms to saddle my horse and I will ride over to The George straight away to talk to Elizabeth's mother.'

Mrs Morris replied, 'Yes Sir, I will do that at once,' and left the room. The groom fetched the horse to the front door; Mr Jonathon mounted his horse and rode off towards the George.

He arrived at the inn to the sound of a drum banging; outside the George were a number of soldiers, resplendent in their red uniforms. A Sergeant was standing on the back of a cart talking to the crowd of men that had gathered. He was telling the crowd he was there to recruit men to fight Napoleon and, if there were any good men there who would like three meals a day and a pension after twenty-one years, he would be very pleased to give them the King's shilling.

There were about ten or fifteen men listening to him, there was not a lot of work to be had locally so it seemed a good proposition. The Sergeant told them, as a bonus for every man that took the shilling, there would be a flagon of ale, so if anyone had the courage to fight for their country, now was the time. The Sergeant then jumped off the cart, made his way into the inn where he sat at a table and waited for the first man to sign up to take the King's shilling. One man walked in, signed the paper, took the shilling and was told to sit at another table where he would be given his ale. Six men came forward, signed the paper, took their shilling, sat at the table and were given their ale.

Jonathon watched the proceedings with great interest, some of the men had more ale and, by the time the Sergeant told them it was time to climb aboard the cart to go to the barracks, some of them were very unsteady on their legs! He watched them drive off and thought there were six good men there, he hoped they would be safe.

He went into the inn and asked one of the serving maids if he could speak to Meg. The maid went to fetch Meg, who was surprised to see Jonathon and greeted him warmly, 'Mr Jonathon, Sir. We have not seen you here in many years, since you first came to ask about Elizabeth having lessons with Annabelle. I trust all is well?'

Jonathon replied, 'It is about these arrangements that I have come to talk to you.'

Meg asked him to come through to the parlour so they could have a discussion in private. Jonathon followed her and sat down, he looked at Meg and began, 'I have a proposition for you. I wondered if it would be possible for Elizabeth to come and stay at the Manor to keep Annabelle company. Annabelle has nobody of her own age and it would help both of them to study together.'

Meg looked at him, her mind racing with the implications of his proposal, 'I really do not know. I enjoy having Elizabeth here. She is a good girl and helps me a lot and she is good company.'

Jonathon said, 'I do appreciate how you feel but I think it would be an advantage if she could stop as she will continue to receive a good education and they both enjoy each other's company so much. She is already being taught everything she will need in life and I will make sure she is treated well.'

Meg looked at him, 'Yes, I can see all the advantages of this plan and I know she is receiving a good education but I feel I am losing my daughter.'

'You do know I lost my wife in an accident and Annabelle lost her mother. She has never stopped missing her and I think a companion would help her.'

Meg replied, 'I can understand how you feel. When Meg comes home tonight I will talk to her and make sure this is what she wants. She can bring her things back with her tomorrow and we can see how it will all work out.'

Jonathon turned to Meg, 'Thank you for your kindness and courtesy. I think it will all work out, of course, only time will tell us.' He touched his hat and walked out of the inn, one of the ostlers brought his horse to the door.

When he arrived back at the manor, one of the grooms took his horse back to the stable. He asked one of the footmen to fetch Mrs Morris as he wanted to discuss something with her. Mrs Morris appeared and Jonathon told her Elizabeth would, in fact, be coming to stay for a while so to make sure the bedroom would be ready for tomorrow. He looked at Mrs Morris, 'I would like you to teach the girls how to cook as I think it is an advantage for young ladies to know how to cook.'

'You want me to teach Miss Elizabeth as well?'

'Yes, I want both of them to learn how to cook. I also want you to send for the seamstress as both of them will need a dress for the ball. Miss Elizabeth will also need a riding habit as I will ask Mr Potts to give her riding lessons.' Mrs Morris left to carry out her tasks.

Mr Jonathon went up to the nursery and knocked on the door, Annabelle and Elizabeth were having their lessons so he apologized to Miss Jones and said he needed to speak to the girls. He told Elizabeth he had been to see her mother at the inn and she agreed with the arrangement for Elizabeth to stay for a short while and to see if the arrangement suited everyone. 'In the meantime,' he continued, 'When you have finished your lessons with Miss Jones, I would like Mr Potts to give you riding lessons.' He smiled at both of them and left the room.

As he walked away he remembered the other thing he was going to say, he returned and told them he had instructed the seamstress to come and measure them for ball gowns and a riding habit for Elizabeth. He turned and left, leaving two girls with big smiles on their faces.

The seamstress arrived the following day, her name was Miss Cope and she had made dresses and outfits for the gentry for many years and she took pride in the work she did. Mrs Morris took her up to the nursery for her to meet the two young ladies. Mrs Morris introduced her to Annabelle and Elizabeth and said she would leave her with the girls, as she knew the measuring of new clothes would take a while. In the meantime, she would send a tray of tea up for Miss Cope.

Miss Cope had brought a large bag with samples and patterns and she told the girls to look through the samples and then tell her which ones they liked. The girls were intrigued by the patterns and the colours and they spent a long time deciding on the ones they liked. Annabelle pulled out some gold material and said she liked that, Miss Cope told her to look again so she was sure which material she liked as once the dress was made it would be too late for her to change her mind.

Annabelle looked again at the materials and she found a lovely peach silk, Miss Cope told her she thought that would be more suitable for her. She then looked at Elizabeth and asked her to choose one for herself, Elizabeth found a lovely blue silk material and told Miss Cope she had found the one she liked and did not think she needed to look any further. Miss Cope told them both they had made good choices and she would make a nice dress each for them.

She asked for a stool for the girls to stand on so she could measure them. She then told them she would draw a sketch so they could see the design of the dresses. First, she measured Annabelle and she told her she would put a false hem on the dress to allow for growth. Then Elizabeth's turn came and she stood on the stool to be measured. The seamstress told the girls she had about three weeks before the ball and that should be plenty of time. She said she would be back in a fortnight's time for a fitting of the dresses to make sure they would look perfect on the night of the ball.

Miss Cope told Elizabeth she also had to make a riding habit for her; it would have a full skirt, as she would need to ride sidesaddle. The material would be heavy-duty wool, as when she would be riding in the winter she would need a heavy-duty cloth to keep her warm. She told Elizabeth she would make a hat to go with the outfit too; Miss Cope was a very clever seamstress, she was a very capable woman with a talent in her hands and she knew what she was doing. She loved her work, as she liked to see the dresses when they were finished.

Next day Mrs Morris the housekeeper said to Elizabeth that Mr Potts wanted to see her and Miss Annabelle in the stables as he wanted to start the riding lessons. Elizabeth and Annabelle went down to the stable block to find him. He told Elizabeth he had instructions from Mr Jonathon to teach her to ride and he also thought it would be a good idea if Annabelle joined them as it would be company for Elizabeth and horses also liked company.

Mr Potts had two horses waiting for them; they were Welsh cobs and they were fifteen hands high and had nice temperaments. He told the girls he would teach them every aspect of riding from saddling the horses to grooming them when they had finished riding them. He would show them so, if they were unfortunate enough to have one of the buckles come undone, they would have enough knowledge to put it right. He told them he would saddle one of the cobs first and then they could try.

He fetched one of the cobs, took the bridle off, opened the horse's mouth, put the bit in and put the bridle over the top of the ears then told them to make sure the bridle was firm but not too tight or you would give the horse a sore mouth. He told them the halter you put on the horse must be the right size for the horse's head, not too tight and not too loose, as everyone must be comfortable when they ride, including the horse. He then turned to the saddle, first you put a protective rug over the horse; then put the saddle on. The straps go under the girth and you tighten them up; not too tight but enough to keep the saddle in place. He told them the stirrups should be measured for the length of your leg, so it was comfortable to ride. This part of the lesson took about an hour to explain and demonstrate to the girls and, at the end of the hour, Elizabeth had learnt a lot from a man who had an abundance of knowledge and was willing to pass it on.

Mr Potts then told them they would lead the horses down to the paddock and there they could get the feel of the horses. Annabelle was an accomplished horsewoman as she had ridden since she was a small child, but Elizabeth, although she had been taught to ride at the inn by her brother Noah, had not ridden much since then and would need a lot of instruction.

They made their way down to the paddock; Mr Potts showed Elizabeth how to mount the pony and showed her how to canter round the paddock until she had found her seat. They rode round the paddock and Elizabeth soon picked up the rhythm again. Mr Potts walked over to Elizabeth and told her she had the reins too tight and to give the horse a little bit of leeway so the horse could enjoy the canter. An hour went by and Elizabeth was regaining some confidence so Mr Potts told them he would fetch his horse and they could have a ride in the park. He told Elizabeth he would not put a lead rein on her horse, as she seemed to have settled back into the rhythm of riding very well.

They all went into the park, the two girls led the way and Mr Potts followed behind to keep an eye on them. After another hour, Mr Potts told them it was time to go back as the horses were becoming tired. They returned to the stable yard and Elizabeth and Annabelle dismounted. Mr Potts told them this was now the important part, you must never give your horse a drink of water until they have cooled down as otherwise they can develop colic. The groom came over and they were showed how to rub them down with straw, put a blanket on them, and wait for them to cool down. After an hour, they could then give them a drink of water. Mr Potts told the girls that was the lesson for the day and he hoped they had enjoyed it, the girls told him they had enjoyed themselves very much and thanked him for his patience.

A couple of weeks went by and Miss Cope arrived at Hough Manor with the dresses. The girls were very excited when they saw Miss Cope take the large bags up to the nursery. She said to the girls, 'Annabelle, this is yours. Take it to your bedroom and put the dress on then come back to the nursery so I can make sure it fits properly.' Annabelle took the dress, went to her bedroom and changed. When she looked in the mirror, she was very pleased with the dress. She went back to the nursery and Miss Cope told her she did not think she would have to make any alterations, as the fit was perfect. Annabelle thanked her very much for all her hard work.

Miss Cope then turned to Elizabeth and told her to go and try her dress on; Elizabeth took the dress to her bedroom and put it on. She looked at herself in the mirror, she was very pleased with her reflection and thought how lovely the dress was and how grown up it made her look. She felt comfortable in it and thought she would have a lovely time at the ball. She went along to the nursery; Miss Cope looked at Elizabeth and told her she would not need to alter any of her dress either as it fitted well. Elizabeth went back to her bedroom, changed out of the dress, and took it back to the nursery. Miss Cope then gave her the riding habit so she could go and try it on. She went back to her bedroom and tried the habit on and again it fitted perfectly, the hat had a feather on it and the whole outfit made her look a lot older than she was and she was very pleased with it too. Elizabeth returned to Annabelle and Miss Cope in the nursery. Miss Cope told Elizabeth and Annabelle she was satisfied with the work as long as the young ladies were. They both told her they were very pleased and thanked her very much.

CHAPTER 11

The Hunt Ball

After the dresses had arrived, the time for the ball was getting very close. It was the highlight of the year at Hough Manor and everything had to be perfect, all the county gentry came for this event so it was important Hough Manor looked its best. The servants cleaned and polished the Manor until it sparkled. Mrs Morris usually took charge of all the arrangements for the hunt ball and the house had to be cleaned from top to bottom. Mrs Morris was a good organiser and she knew all that was required. Plans went ahead to decorate the Manor for the ball; the gardener was asked to bring in greenery for the decorations; the cook was instructed on the menu for the seventy guests.

The gardeners brought in logs for the fires; they were apple wood and always made the Manor smell welcoming. The beeswax candles burned brightly and lit the room with a warm glow.

Hough Manor's delicacy was roast suckling pigs, two of them were roasted along with chickens, pheasants and partridges. A large ham was cooked, eggs in aspic and many other dishes. A sweet course followed which included syllabub, apple cream, sippet pudding, cakes and a variety of cheeses, including potted cheese. Mr Jonathon was renowned throughout the county for his generosity and the good table he provided, he had one of the largest estates in the county and so felt he should provide a high standard of entertaining. All the silver had been cleaned and everything was under control. Mr Jonathon knew Mrs

Morris was a very capable housekeeper and he could leave all the arrangements in her hands.

The night of the Hunt Ball arrived; Elizabeth and Annabelle dressed with the help of one of the maids, who also styled their hair. Both of them felt very sophisticated, Elizabeth went to Annabelle's room where they paraded in front of the big mirror. They both felt very excited and grown up, then they went downstairs to show Annabelle's father. Mr Jonathon said he would like both of them to be in the hallway to greet the guests and welcome them to Hough Manor.

The musicians arrived and took their places in the main hall and started to play; the footmen were in the main hall with trays of drinks to welcome the guests. The first guest arrived and Mr Jonathon greeted them and presented the two young ladies and that was the start of the evening. Mr Jonathon, Annabelle and Elizabeth greeted all the guests until the last one had arrived and the Great Hall was full of people. All the men were in their evening dress and all the ladies in their ball gowns, it looked a splendid affair and everything was going to plan.

The musicians started to play a waltz and Annabelle's father asked her if she would do him the honour of leading the dancing, she said she would be honoured to. Elizabeth watched as they started dancing and thought what a lovely sight it was. Unbeknown to Elizabeth, two young men were watching her across the ballroom, they both started to walk over to her but the one who reached her first asked if he could introduce himself. He told her he lived on the other side of the county and he would like to make her acquaintance, he said his name was Damon Hiskin. The other young man, John Kemp, realised he would have to wait for the next dance to become acquainted with Elizabeth. 'My name is Elizabeth,' she replied to Damon.

He smiled at her, 'That is a very pretty name. May I have the honour of the next dance with you?'

Elizabeth replied, 'Yes, I would like that very much.'

Damon escorted Elizabeth onto the dance floor; they made a striking couple as they waltzed around the floor. Too soon, the music stopped and Damon escorted Elizabeth back to her seat, he told her he had enjoyed dancing with her and would return to dance with her again, if she consented. She smilingly agreed.

During the evening, the butler went into the ballroom, blew the hunting horn, and informed all the guests that refreshments were being served if they wished to make their way to the dining room. Slowly people made their way there, the food had been set out on the long table and it looked magnificent, there were large hams, chickens, pheasants, the centrepiece of the roast suckling pigs and for dessert syllabub, apple cream, sippet pudding, individual sweet tarts – the cook had excelled herself. Hough Manor had a reputation throughout the county for its excellent Hunt suppers and everyone tucked in with gusto.

As Annabelle and Elizabeth went into supper and they were looking at the supper table, Damon approached and said, 'Hello, we bump into each other again.' Elizabeth smiled at him and she introduced Annabelle. Damon told Annabelle it was a pleasure to meet her and how much he was enjoying the evening. He then turned to Elizabeth and asked her if he could have the pleasure of another dance after supper. 'Yes, I would be very pleased to,' Elizabeth replied.

After the refreshments, the girls went back into the Great Hall and stood watching the dancers. Damon came across to Elizabeth, 'I believe you promised me this dance,' so she smiled at him, 'Yes, I believe I did.' Damon escorted her onto the dance floor, they made a handsome couple as they danced but too soon the dance finished and Damon escorted her back to her seat. He asked if he could sit and talk for a while, she replied, 'If you would wish, Sir.' So he sat down and began by asking if she lived at Hough Manor. Elizabeth told him she lived at the Manor with Annabelle and Mr Jonathon. Damon told her it was a beautiful house and asked whether she was happy living here. She replied that she was very happy; he then asked her if she could ride. Elizabeth told him she did ride and had been having lessons with Mr Potts as she wanted to become an accomplished horsewoman if she could, 'Mr Potts is a good teacher and I am learning a great deal.' Damon asked if she had a horse, she told him she had and he asked her the name of the horse. 'Rainbow is his name,' she answered. Damon thought that was a lovely name and asked if he was a big horse.

Elizabeth replied, 'Yes, he is sixteen hands and is a hunter.'

'I would very much like to see him,' Damon said.

Elizabeth told him they could walk down to the stables and he could see for himself. They left by the side door and walked down to the stable yard and into the stables. She told Damon that Rainbow was in the loose box at the end if he would like to follow her. Damon tried to take Elizabeth's hand but she kept her hands clasped together so he could not.

They reached Rainbow's stall and he came straight to Elizabeth, snickering with delight. The horse then noticed Elizabeth had company and neighed in fright, as he had never seen Damon before. Elizabeth told Damon to stand back as the horse was nervous of strangers. Damon told her he was a horseman, he understood horses, they responded to discipline and so would Rainbow.

Elizabeth told him, 'He needs to be treated gently. He does not want any discipline, all he needs is love.' Rainbow was becoming very agitated in the loose box and Damon repeated, 'The horse needs some discipline.' Again Elizabeth disagreed with him, Damon then caught hold of her and tried to kiss her. She pushed him away and said, 'Go away, Sir, you forget your manners,' but he carried on trying to pull Elizabeth to him, ripping her dress as he did so. The horse started kicking at the loose box and neighing, Elizabeth started screaming. The noise was horrendous and the grooms, who lived over the stables, heard and hastened to see what the commotion was about.

Once they saw the situation, the head groom went straight to the house to fetch Mr Jonathon and told him there was a disturbance in the stables. They hastened back to find Elizabeth crying in a corner and the stable hands guarding Damon, the horse was still very agitated. Mr Jonathon took in the scene and asked Damon what he thought he was doing. He replied, 'I was only being friendly.'

Mr Jonathon looked at him, 'I think you were trying to be more than friendly.' He went into one of the tack rooms, fetched a riding crop and struck Damon across the face and told him to leave the premises and never return as he would no longer be welcome in his house. Damon went for Jonathon, but he was not quick enough, Jonathon struck him again and again with the riding crop, until Damon decided he had met his match and thought it was time he left.

The nearest exit was at the end of the stable block, he ran towards where his horse was stabled but Jonathon ran after him, thrashing him with the crop as he went. Damon managed to put his foot in the stirrup but the horse panicked with all the noise and bolted across the stable yard. Damon was only half mounted; he could not release himself and was dragged across the yard, but the horse kept going. The grooms saw the situation and managed to catch the horse by the halter. By this stage, the commotion had been heard in the house and the guests came out to see what the rumpus was about.

Damon was unconscious on the cobbled yard; the grooms had released his foot from the stirrup. Mr Jonathon went to him, he told the grooms to lift him up and take him into the harness room to see what the damage was. They took him in and laid him on the table. Mr Jonathon told one of the grooms to go to the house and ask the doctor to attend. The groom found Dr West and asked him to come immediately, as there had been an accident. He nodded to the groom and both of them hastened to the stables. Mr Jonathon thanked the doctor for coming and told him they needed his assistance as there had been a mishap, but the doctor looked at the figure lying on the table and said, 'You don't need my assistance. The man is dead, you need an undertaker.'

A gasp went round the men in the stable. Mr Jonathon said to one of the grooms, 'You had better go over to Damon Hiskin's home and tell them there has been a terrible accident, that Damon is dead.' The groom left immediately to break the tragic news.

Jonathon stood for a moment, it was a terrible end to a lovely evening. He told Elizabeth to find Annabelle and go up to their rooms and he would see them later on. He walked very slowly back to the house and made his way to the ballroom where the musicians were still playing. He asked them to stop and stood in front of his guests to make an announcement, 'Ladies and gentlemen, there has been a terrible accident, Damon Hiskin has died. In the circumstances, I think it would be appropriate if we ended the festivities and you all made your way home.'

John Kemp had watched the drama unfold and thought to

himself that if he had reached Elizabeth first, none of this tragedy would have happened.

Dr West came into the house and went into the hall, seeking Jonathon. He said that he would like a private word with him so Jonathon took the doctor into the library. Dr West told him he would have to inform the Sheriff of the sudden death and there would doubtless be an inquiry as to how he had died. Jonathon was taken aback, 'I do not understand, it was just a tragic accident. I hope there will not be problems.'

Dr West looked at him, 'I have to inform the Sheriff and it will be taken out of my hands as it is a sudden death. If you would excuse me now, I will make my way home. It has been a very sad end to a lovely evening.'

Dr West left and Jonathon went back to the stables to see the grooms, they were shocked and still standing about, unsure what to do with themselves. Someone had covered the body over with a blanket to await the undertaker. Jonathon told them it had been a very sad evening and he had come to see what was happening in the stables. The grooms said that Rainbow was still very upset and could not seem to settle. Jonathon asked one of them to go into the house and get Mrs Morris to fetch Miss Elizabeth and ask her to come to the stable as the horse was still very upset. Elizabeth put her cloak on, as it was now very cold outside, and came down at once. She made her way with the groom to the stables and, as they walked along the corridor, Rainbow put his head over his stall door. As soon as he saw Elizabeth, he neighed and snickered with delight and quickly became calm. The grooms watched in amazement as they had never seen anything like this, Rainbow was calm: it seemed Elizabeth could do anything with him. He was obviously a one-owner horse. Jonathon was also looking on in astonishment.

The grooms asked him what should they do now but he said nothing more could be done that night and tomorrow would be a busy day with the Sheriff and the undertaker coming, so they should all return to their beds. There would be an investigation into the cause of Damon's death and they would all be required to give a statement. He told Elizabeth to finish settling Rainbow and then they would return to the house.

On the way back, Elizabeth looked at Jonathon, 'I am sorry for all the trouble that has happened tonight and spoilt the hunt ball.'

'It was not of your making, Elizabeth. It was the fault of a very silly man who has brought about this tragic event and brought great sorrow to his family. He abused my hospitality, tried to abuse you and now has paid a terrible price.'

They walked back to the house; Jonathon told Elizabeth they should all try to get some sleep, as tomorrow would be a very busy day. Annabelle had waited for them and she agreed it would be a very difficult day for them all. They all made their way to their bedrooms; each hoping sleep would come.

CHAPTER 12

The Trial

Jonathon arose early, as he knew it would be a very difficult day. As he was eating his breakfast, Mrs Morris came to tell him Mr and Mrs Hiskin were in the hall and would like to see him. Jonathon walked into the hall, shook hands with Mr Hiskin and took them into the drawing room. He told them how very sorry he was on this sad occasion. Mr Hiskin told him he did not want any sympathy; he wanted to know the facts surrounding his son's death. Jonathon explained how his son had tried to mount his horse, caught his foot in the stirrup and the horse had bolted. He could not release himself from the stirrup and was dragged along over the cobbled yard.

Mr Hiskin looked at Jonathon and said, 'According to Dr West, there was a considerable number of marks on my son and I would like to know how those occurred.'

Jonathon said, 'Yes, there were a lot of whip marks on your son. We did have a confrontation but if I tell you exactly what the situation was it will be hurt on top of hurt.'

Mr Hiskin replied, 'I want the truth of what happened and what went wrong and if you were in my shoes you would want to know the truth.'

Jonathon realised he would have to tell the truth no matter how hurtful and explained, 'The truth of the matter is that your son tried to take advantage of Elizabeth, my daughter's young companion. I interfered and took a riding whip to him so he tried to run away. That is when he tried to mount his horse, the horse took fright, bolted and dragged your son along with him across the yard. That is how this terrible tragedy happened.'

Mr Hiskin looked shocked and said, 'I am not satisfied with this explanation and I am sure the Sheriff will have questions to ask. You may be landed gentry in this area but we still have some law and you will need to answer to the Sheriff. I will take my son's body now and I hope in my lifetime I never see you again, you have given us a great deal of sorrow and I think your explanation needs looking at by the Sheriff.' He turned on his heel and walked out; he gently put his son's body on the cart and drove off along the lane.

A few days went by and the Sheriff arrived and asked to see Mr Jonathon. The Sheriff told Mr Jonathon there had been a complaint, which Jonathon said he was fully expecting, and asked him and his assistant to go with him into the library. He offered them refreshments, which they declined.

The Sheriff then asked Jonathon to give him a full explanation of the incident. Jonathon gave a precise account of the events leading up to the tragic death of Damon Hiskin. The Sheriff listened fully to Jonathon, making notes as the story unfolded. He looked at Jonathon, 'I will report all this to the Magistrate and he will decide if there is any action to be taken. This is obviously a very serious matter as a man has died. The Magistrate will decide on a course of action as a death certificate will need to be issued with cause of death stated before a burial can take place.' Mr Jonathon knew the matter was serious; he showed the Sheriff and his assistant to the door and watched them drive down the drive, pondering on the outcome of the meeting.

Two weeks later a constable arrived at Hough Manor asking for Mr Jonathon and Elizabeth; he waited in the hall for them to come down. Mr Jonathon came downstairs and asked him if he could help. The constable explained he had a summons to serve as the Magistrates felt they had enough evidence for a court hearing on a charge of assault. Jonathon sent one of the footmen to fetch Miss Elizabeth as the constable also wanted to talk to her. Miss Elizabeth came downstairs and joined them in the library. The constable looked uncomfortable and told her he did not want upset her but she had been summoned to court to give evidence about Mr Hiskin's death, as she was a witness and Mr Jonathon Grantham had been summoned on a charge of assault. Elizabeth asked the constable what it all meant so he explained to her that, in the cases of sudden, unexplained death, an investigation had to be carried out before a death certificate could be issued as the cause of death had to be determined before a funeral could take place. The constable left, and Jonathon looked at Elizabeth and told her he thought they should go and see his lawyer Mr Grant in the morning so would she be ready first thing tomorrow.

Next morning, both Elizabeth and Jonathon were ready to leave after an early breakfast; the coach drew up at the front door and they both stepped in and set off. The coach arrived in the middle of town as Mr Grant's chambers were in the main square. They climbed the rickety stairs to where the clerk was waiting for them and he showed them into the office. It was a large room, filled with bookcases and rows of books.

Mr Grant sat behind a very large desk; he came forward to shake Jonathon's hand and told him it was nice to meet him again. Jonathon introduced Elizabeth to Mr Grant; he shook Elizabeth's hand and told her it was a pleasure to meet her. He indicated for Jonathon and Elizabeth to be seated and then asked them of what service he could be to them. Jonathon looked at him, 'Unfortunately we had an accident at the Hough; I expect you have heard about it. There was an unfortunate death and the Magistrate has summoned both Elizabeth and me to appear in court, myself on an assault charge and Elizabeth as a witness. We have come to see you in the hope that you will represent us in this matter.'

Mr Grant told him he would, and then he asked Jonathon to tell him exactly what did occur on that night. Jonathon related the events of that evening in full detail. Mr Grant listened very carefully to Jonathon, he sat forward in his chair and rested his chin on his hand and watched Jonathon closely as he listened to his account of the tragic night.

Mr Grant remained silent for a few minutes, gazing out of the window, deep in thought, and then he looked at Jonathon, 'Let us look at the worst possibility, this man died at Hough Manor trying to escape from you. They could bring a charge of manslaughter, but as they are charging you with assault that would not appear to be the case. The difficulty in this case is that we have only two witnesses, Elizabeth being the main one, so therefore it is important we deliver her evidence very clearly.'

He then said he would like Elizabeth to go with his clerk and give a very clear account of the events of the night so the clerk could write down every piece of information. He rang the bell and his clerk appeared, he explained that he would like him to listen to Elizabeth's record of events and to write everything down. The clerk showed Elizabeth into his room so the events could be recorded.

Mr Grant looked at Jonathon, 'This is serious but not that serious that we can't find a solution. The difficulty is being landed gentry, as there is a lot of jealousy and animosity in this county at the minute. We will have to put up a good defence for you and, in my opinion, the worst thing that could happen is you could be sent to prison for two years or, in the extreme case, you could be deported. I do not think we need to go down that road, I think your best defence is that you defended the honour of one of the young ladies in your household, I think the jury would take that into consideration. I would like you to write down the events of that night in full detail, leaving nothing out, and then I will go through the statement with you, because we want to make sure we have not missed anything out. I think Mr Hiskin has brought the case as he wants revenge for his son's death.'

Mr Grant told Jonathon he wanted two copies of his statement, one for himself and one for Jonathon. Furthermore, he told Jonathon he wanted him to read his statement every day so he had the events firmly in his mind. Miss Elizabeth should also have a copy of her statement and read it every day. He looked at Jonathon, 'I know you think that is extreme but being in court is very daunting but doing this means you should make no mistakes with your evidence. You will then remember clearly everything that happened and not muddle the information. The jury will take that into account. I do not think we need to meet again. You will both have your statements to study. On the day of the case, we will meet here in chambers an hour before the case starts to refresh ourselves on the evidence.'

Jonathon thought Mr Grant was a very competent lawyer and he was fortunate to have his services. Jonathon noticed that Elizabeth looked very frightened and worried and said, 'You have nothing to worry about. You have done nothing wrong; the harm was done to you. If there is any law and justice in this country then we have nothing to worry about.'

Mr Grant told Jonathon he wanted to see the other witness

so asked him to instruct the groom to come see him and make a statement. This would be important for the case as he did not want to leave any stone unturned and he wanted to put a good case to the jury. Jonathon agreed and thought what a shrewd man he was and knew Mr Grant was more than capable of handling the case.

Jonathon stood up shook hands with Mr Grant, thanked him for his support, and said he would see him on the day of the court hearing.

Mr Grant said, 'Mr Jonathon, we will put the best defence possible and I am sure the outcome will be favourable.'

Elizabeth came forward and shook Mr Grant's hand, 'Thank you, Sir.'

Mr Grant looked at her, 'That is a pleasure, Miss.'

As Jonathon led the way back down the stairs, he told Elizabeth he thought they should go for some refreshments and the best inn in the town was The Dragon. 'We will go there and have a meal as we have been a long time here at the lawyers and it is a long drive back to Hough Manor.'

They stepped down into the street and walked along until they came to The Dragon. Jonathon led the way inside and went into a small side room where the gentry usually sat. A serving maid came to them and he asked for a table for two. The maid showed them to a table set for two people, Jonathon made sure Elizabeth was comfortable and then went quickly to tell the coachman to have his own meal and to put the price of the meal on Jonathon's tally. The coachman thanked him very much and Jonathon returned to Elizabeth.

The serving maid returned and told them the special of the house was hung mutton and it was very tasty. Jonathon asked Elizabeth if she would like that and she said she would like it very much. The mutton arrived with plenty of vegetables and smelled delicious, they were both hungry and tucked into the meal with much appreciation.

Once the meal was finished, they were brought two coffees and while they were savouring those, a gentleman approached their table. He greeted Jonathon and said, 'Hello, I did not expect to see you here.' Jonathon told him they were there on some business and the man replied, 'I am sorry to hear about your sorrow at the Hunt Ball. You could well do without that, sorrow never knocks at anyone's door, it comes in uninvited.'

Jonathon agreed with him and then said, 'Allow me to introduce this young lady. Her name is Elizabeth and she is the companion of my young daughter, Annabelle.' He said to Elizabeth, 'This gentleman is John Kemp.'

The young man stepped forward and shook Elizabeth's hand, 'Pleased to meet you, I hope you enjoy your meal and I hope one day we will meet again.' Elizabeth thought he was a very pleasant looking young man with nice manners. He shook Jonathan's hand and left. Jonathon told Elizabeth that John Kemp's family were merchants and they dealt in all manner of goods. They lived on the other side of the county.

Jonathon said to Elizabeth, 'It is time we set off as it is getting dark and late. I will go and tell the coachman we are ready.' Elizabeth told him she had enjoyed the meal and the day to which Jonathon replied that the day would have been better if they had not come on such a sad errand.

Elizabeth said, 'Life is like that: it is very unfair on occasions and then it gives us a sprinkle of happiness.' Jonathon looked at her and realised how grown up she had become; she was a young lady now. The coach arrived at the door, they got in and set off on their way back to Hough Manor.

A month went by and the Sheriff delivered a summons to Jonathon to attend the court. Elizabeth also received a summons to attend as a witness. Jonathon told Elizabeth he thought it would be a good idea if they started early for town so as to arrive in good time. He also thought it would be a good idea if Annabelle came with them; she would be good company for Elizabeth as it would be a long day.

The morning of the trial arrived, the coach was brought around and they all got in and made their way to town. As they arrived in the town, there seemed to be many people outside the courthouse. They arrived at the chambers of Mr Grant, he ushered them inside and took them into his office to discuss the tactics of the day. Jonathon introduced Annabelle to him as he had not met her before. The lawyer asked Jonathon and Elizabeth if they had read their statements thoroughly and were conversant with them; they both told him they were.

Mr Grant then said, 'We are well-prepared; I will now explain to you how proceedings take place. We shall go to court and Mr Jonathon will stand in the dock and you, Elizabeth, will sit outside the court until you are called. Annabelle, you will be sitting inside.' He continued his explanation then asked if either of them had any questions but Jonathon said, 'No, there is nothing I need to ask. This is just a very unfortunate situation I find myself in.'

Mr Grant replied, 'We can deal with this; we are fortunate there is only the one charge of assault.' He suggested they should walk to the courthouse as it was not very far. They set off for the court and as they approached, people recognised Mr Jonathon and started to shout and jeer at him. Jonathon looked at them and thought they had judged him before all the correct facts became public and had condemned him before the trial, but he thought that is how life is. They made their way through the crowd and went up the steps of the courthouse.

After some formalities, Jonathon was taken through to the dock. Mr Grant was sitting in front of him and he turned to Jonathon and said, 'We will have justice.' The Clerk of the Court stood as the jury filed in and took their places, then the Clerk asked everyone to stand as the judge, His Worship Lord Pierce, entered. The Clerk then told everyone to sit and said the court was now in session for the case of Jonathon Grantham. The prosecution lawyer stood and told the court he was representing the Hiskin family on the events of that night. He turned to Jonathon and asked him to relate the events of the night of the occurrence. As Jonathon related the events of the night, the lawyer interrupted him and said, 'You took a riding crop to him?'

Jonathon said, 'Yes, I did.'

The lawyer replied, 'Do you think that was an honourable thing to do, to take a riding crop to one of your guests?'

Jonathon replied, 'Yes, I do. That man had abused a young lady and abused my hospitality and I was right to do that.'

The lawyer looked at Jonathon, 'Were you right to take a man's life?'

'I did not take his life. Circumstances on that night lost him his life and if he had not been such a bounder this would have never happened.'

The lawyer said, 'Could you have not dealt with the situation in a better fashion?'

Jonathon replied, 'We can all deal with situations differently in hindsight. I am sorry for his death but the majority of the sadness he brought onto himself.'

The lawyer came back at Jonathon, 'When he was running

away from you along the stable corridor did you think he had had enough punishment?'

Jonathon replied, 'Nobody was thinking that at the time, I was angry for his behaviour to a young lady but, at that point, I was leaving him to make his escape.'

'Could nobody have stopped the horse?'

'It all happened so quickly, the horse bolted before anyone could do anything and the accident happened,' Jonathon replied.

The lawyer said, 'No more questions.'

Mr Grant then stood up to ask his questions. 'Mr Jonathon, how old is your ward?'

'She is seventeen, Sir,' he replied.

'Is that the first ball she has attended?'

'I believe so,' replied Jonathon.

Mr Grant looked at Jonathon, 'I would like you tell us exactly what happened that night.'

Jonathon looked round the court, 'I was alerted by one of the grooms who said that there was a fracas in the stables. I went down to the stables and there was Elizabeth in a corner crying, with her dress torn. There was Hiskin standing there, the horse was in the loose box, it was very agitated and was kicking the loosebox door. It was a very unpleasant situation. I saw what he had done to an innocent girl, with a torn dress and I thought to myself how could a man do that to a young girl and I lost my temper.'

'You lost your temper, Mr Jonathon?' asked the lawyer.

'Yes, I did. How could any man do that to a young girl at her first ball? I am not ashamed; any man would have done the same.'

Mr Grant said, 'Any other man.'

Jonathon replied, 'Any decent man would have done the same. It was an occasion for action, to do what was right and I believe I did the right thing. I protected a young lady who had been abused, tricked into the stables by an unscrupulous man.'

Mr Grant looked round the court, 'I have no further questions for Mr Jonathon.'

The Judge asked the Prosecution if there were any further questions, he replied, 'No Sir, no further questions.' The Clerk of the court then called Elizabeth as the first witness, 'Elizabeth Jolly to the stand.'

The usher escorted Elizabeth to the witness box, all eyes were upon her as she stepped up and was handed the Bible and took the oath to tell the truth. Elizabeth was trembling and felt very frightened but the Judge looked at her with compassion, 'Nobody will harm you, young lady. All we want is for you to tell us the truth about the incident on the night of the ball.'

The lawyer for the prosecution stood up and asked to Elizabeth, 'Why did you go down to the stables with a man you hardly knew, to look at a horse in the middle of a ball?'

Elizabeth looked straight at the lawyer, 'Damon Hiskin appeared to me to be a nice man and he appeared to be interested in Rainbow, my horse, and he asked to look at him. I did not believe he had other intentions, I believed what he said. To my distress, I found out that was a lie.'

'That was a lie,' the lawyer repeated.

'Yes, that was a lie. I did not give him any encouragement at all, he terrified me. He backed me into the corner of the loosebox and tried to take advantage of me. I have never been so scared in all my life. I had never been treated like that before in my life. No gentleman I had ever met before had ever treated me like that. I was completely deceived and it was only that Mr Jonathon came so quickly that prevented me from being in greater danger.'

The lawyer for the prosecution said, 'No more questions,' and sat down.

Mr Grant then stood up, 'I would like to question the young lady.' He looked at Elizabeth, 'May I call you Elizabeth?'

'Yes, Sir,' she replied.

'What is your position at Hough Manor?'

'I am Miss Annabelle's companion,' she replied.

'Regarding the ball, is that the first time you have been to a ball?'

'Yes,' Elizabeth replied.

'Have you ever had any associations with any other men?'

'No,' replied Elizabeth.

'Have you ever danced with any other men?'

'No,' she replied, 'The only men I have danced with have been Mr Jonathon and Damon Hiskin.'

Mr Grant looked at Elizabeth, 'You have not had a lot of association with men and you are not very experienced in the ways of the world. When Mr Hiskin asked you to show him your horse, you believed him and that his intentions were honourable and he was not going to take advantage of you.'

'Yes, it was a terrible shock. I had been deceived and I was very frightened,' Elizabeth replied.

'No further questions,' Mr Grant said and sat down.

The Judge looked at the prosecution and the defence lawyers and asked them if there were any more questions and they both replied they had no more questions for Elizabeth. The Judge told the jury they could retire and come to a majority verdict then he left the courtroom. The Clerk told the rest of the court to reconvene in an hour.

An hour passed and everyone returned to court, the Judge looked at the foreman of the jury and asked him if a verdict had been reached. The foreman told him a majority verdict had been reached and, when the Judge asked for their decision on Mr Jonathon Grantham, he replied, 'Guilty of assault.'

The Judge looked at Jonathon and said, 'Jonathon Grantham, you have been found guilty of assault which is a very serious matter and which indirectly led to a man losing his life. This is a very serious matter. I am not going to send you to prison but I am going to fine you seventy guineas.'

Jonathon stepped out of the dock and the Clerk of the court came to him and said, 'The fine will have to be paid within fifteen days,' and Mr Jonathon told him it would be. The Clerk then put his hand forward and said, 'It was a correct verdict and, if you take my advice Mr Jonathon, you will put this behind you.' Jonathon looked at him, 'I will take your advice but it will be very difficult.'

Jonathon then rejoined his daughter Annabelle and Elizabeth and told them he thought they should partake of some refreshments before the journey home. As they walked along the street towards the inn, people jeered at them, shook their fists and shouted, 'Murderer!' Jonathon thought to himself, 'In life man judges man, but really God should be the only judge as that is his right. Man should not judge unless they are aware of the full facts.'

They arrived at the steps of The Dragon and walked in. As they did so, John Kemp greeted them, shook Jonathan's hand and said, 'I see the verdict was guilty and it was half right.' Jonathon just looked at him and said, 'Maybe,' and left it at that. John Kemp told him he had booked a table in the parlour, 'as I imagine you would like some privacy, but, if you wish, I could join you for the meal.' Jonathon had not seen him since he and Elizabeth had first visited the lawyer; he was surprised to see him but grateful that not everyone was treating him like a pariah. They walked through and found the table was ready with cutlery and candlesticks. Jonathon turned to John Kemp and said to him, 'It is very kind of you to arrange for us to have a meal in private, Mr Kemp.'

'Please call me John, Mr Kemp sounds too formal now.'

They shook hands and sat down and John said, 'I must confess to you, I have an ulterior motive for arranging luncheon. I wanted to meet your daughter and her companion again, so it is all not one-sided,' they both laughed, which broke the tension of the day.

The meal went well and John Kemp ordered a bottle of wine. When it arrived, he asked the girls if they would like a glass but they both declined. Jonathon and John enjoyed each other's company, they were both honest and forthright men. When the meal came to an end, Jonathon thanked John for the meal and his courtesy and said, 'It has been a very hard day, a very worrying day, but I feel better now I have dined and talked with you.'

John replied, 'I have enjoyed the company of all three you and I would like your permission to call at Hough Manor.'

Jonathon looked surprised but turned to Annabelle and Elizabeth and said, 'Mr Kemp is saying he would like to call on you both.'

The girls looked at each other; both nodded their heads and said, 'Yes.' The day had started out very unpleasant but had ended on an enjoyable note. Jonathon called for his coach; when it arrived at the front door, they all stepped in and set off for home.

CHAPTER 13

John Kemp

They arrived back at Hough Manor and were all pleased to be home. It had been a very tense day but, at the end of the day, someone had shown them great kindness. Jonathon thought to himself that it is not all about money, but about kindness and understanding, and John had shown them kindness that day and he would always remember that.

Time went by at Hough Manor and one day Mrs Morris went up to the nursery where Annabelle and Elizabeth were and told them a coachman in full livery had arrived with parcels, one for Miss Annabelle and one for Miss Elizabeth. Both girls went down to the main hall and each collected their parcel. The coachman left and the girls went into the library and opened their parcels, each had some beautiful embroidered handkerchiefs, they were of exquisite quality and in the parcel there was also a letter. It was from John Kemp and he had written to ask if it would be convenient for him to visit on Thursday afternoon.

If he did not hear from them, he would assume it was convenient and call on Thursday. Annabelle told her father John Kemp had written and asked permission to visit her and Elizabeth on Thursday and she asked him if that was convenient and Jonathon replied that it was.

He said, 'I will be present and we will show him round the stables and the gardens as he likes gardens.' Annabelle was very excited at the prospect of the visit and Elizabeth thought it would be lovely to meet him again as she thought he was a gentle and kind man.

Thursday arrived: Annabelle saw John Kemp riding up the drive, he dismounted and tied his horse to the rail, he rang the bell and one of the footmen opened the door. He told the footman his name and that he was expected. The footman asked him to follow him as Mr Jonathon and the two young ladies were in the sitting room and were waiting for him. He followed the footman into the sitting room where there was a roaring fire and a very nice atmosphere in the room. Mr Jonathon went over to him, shook his hand and welcomed him. When he greeted Annabelle and Elizabeth, they both curtsied and said, 'We are pleased to see you, Mr Kemp,' but he asked them to call him by his Christian name, John, as he would prefer that.

Annabelle blushed, 'Yes, we will call you John then.'

John told them he had brought his portfolio with him as he painted as a hobby and he thought they would be interested in seeing some of his work. Mrs Morris came in with tea and a plentiful supply of cakes and, after enjoying some tea, they looked at the paintings. There were sketches and paintings of horses, pigs, sheep and chickens; Annabelle and Elizabeth looked at them with great interest. He said his favourite subjects were horses and he had painted his own horse, Captain, he thought they might be interested in the picture. He fetched the picture out and it was a lovely painting of a beautiful horse, his hobby obviously gave him a lot of pleasure and he was very skilled at it.

Mr Jonathon was very interested in John's paintings; he thought he had caught the likeness of the animals very well. He asked him how had he started and John replied, 'I wanted to put something on paper that everyone would enjoy and I thought all animals have character so I tried to capture each animal's character and, if you are lucky or skilled enough, you can capture that.'

Jonathon said, 'That is the key word, if you can capture those looks it is then truly a wonderful painting.' John thought the man was good company and that was a bonus.

The afternoon sped by and Jonathon asked John if he would like to look at the horses and the gardens and the orangery. He could see some of their horses and see what he thought of them. John said he would very much like to do that as he it had been a very pleasant afternoon and he was enjoying their company.

Mr Jonathon, Annabelle and Elizabeth led the way through the door out to the stables. Jonathon told him he was very proud of his stables; most of the horses were in loose boxes as he found that a good method. As they walked through, Jonathon showed John Annabelle's horse and then his own horse.

He then explained, 'At the bottom is Rainbow but we will have to be very careful as he is an unpredictable horse, he does not take kindly to people he does not like but shows great affection to the people he does like.'

They all walked down to have a look and Elizabeth told them she would lead the way, as he was used to her. As they approached the loose box, Rainbow's ears pricked up, he knew it was Elizabeth, as he could smell her. Rainbow became excited as Elizabeth drew near; John followed and stood at the door with her. Rainbow nuzzled Elizabeth then, to everyone's surprise, he snickered at John, and nuzzled him too. Elizabeth said, 'He likes you, he is a good judge of character. He certainly lets people know if he does not like them!'

They both laughed and John asked, 'Could we go into the loose box to see him?'

Elizabeth said, 'I think that will be all right; he wants to be friends.'

John looked at the horse, he was a lovely looking animal. All the horse was looking for in life was someone to care for him, Elizabeth did and consequently Rainbow showered her with love. John turned to Elizabeth and asked if he could paint Rainbow and he would like to paint her as well with the horse.

They turned round and left the stable, shutting the door behind them. Jonathon had heard the conversation and said to John, 'So, you want to paint Elizabeth and Rainbow?'

John said, 'Only with your permission,' and Jonathon laughed and said, 'Politeness opens many doors, John, and you have the key to that.' They both laughed as they walked away from the stables.

Jonathon then asked if he would like to see the walled garden and John replied that he would very much like to see it. Jonathon told him there was about an acre of walled garden. As they walked through to the garden, there were three or four gardeners working there and they all stopped to doff their caps to the gentlemen and said good afternoon. Jonathon explained that the garden supplied all the fruit and vegetables for the house so they were self-sufficient. The latest project had been an orangery that had taken eighteen months to complete; Jonathon asked him if he would like to see it. John replied he would so they walked on and into the orangery and there were all the oranges hanging from the branches. John was taken aback and said, 'That is an absolutely amazing sight.'

The visit had gone well and, as they all strolled up the garden path back to the house, John said, 'Thank you for your hospitality, thank you for your courtesy and thank you for agreeing to let me paint Elizabeth and Rainbow.'

Jonathon replied, 'It's a pleasure.'

John looked at Annabelle, 'I hope to return to paint Elizabeth and Rainbow and I hope very much you will join us.'

Annabelle replied, 'I would be delighted.' John shook Jonathon's hand and then shook the young ladies' hands and said farewell. They watched him through the window, mount his horse and ride down the drive. The girls looked at each other and both agreed it had been a lovely day and they had both enjoyed themselves.

A few days later, a letter arrived at Hough Manor addressed to Mr Jonathon. John Kemp had written to say how much he had enjoyed his visit and he hoped to come again and, if it was convenient, he would like to come every Thursday afternoon to paint Elizabeth, Annabelle and Rainbow. Jonathon was very pleased as he thought John Kemp had very good manners.

Arrangements were made so John could come on Thursday afternoons to paint the three of them. The arrangement worked very well and the pictures progressed well. God had given John Kemp a certain talent and, with his experience and love of the subject, there was a certain something in the pictures that could not be defined, he loved painting and some of himself went into the pictures.

The weeks went by; John told Annabelle and Elizabeth that the county fair would be arriving in a week's time, and asked if they would like to go. Mr Jonathon came in and John asked him if he would like to go as well. Jonathon told him he thought he would rather not as it had been a very bad year for him with the accident at Hough Manor and he thought it was best if he stayed away. However, he was quite happy for the girls to go with John, as he knew they would enjoy the fair and he knew they would be safe with him.

On the day, John Kemp arrived with an open landau: as he pulled up at the front door, Annabelle and Elizabeth came out with one of the grooms. The groom pulled the step out on the landau and helped the two young ladies to climb in. John said that, as it was a nice day, he did not think they would need the travelling rug but it was there if they felt cold. They all set off for the fair and it was a day to enjoy; the two greys pulled the landau well and the coachman was well experienced in handling them.

As they neared the county fairground, there were many people on the road all heading for the fair, people herding their geese, ducks and other livestock. The sight of all the people fascinated the two girls; they watched two men leading two horses in amongst the crowd, all going to the county fair, all of them taking their animals to trade or to buy. John Kemp told the coachman as they all alighted that he could bring the coach back at four o'clock and meet them in the same place.

The coach drove off, leaving them all to start exploring; as they walked through the fair, there were stalls selling everything you could ever think of. They all marvelled at the sights, sounds and smell of the fair. As they walked along, they came across a stall selling ribbons and hats and John asked them if they would like to look at them. Both the girls said yes they would, they enjoyed looking at the different ribbons, marvelling at all the different colours. John asked if they would like some ribbons for their hair so they both chose some ribbons, each choosing different colours: Annabelle chose red and Elizabeth chose green. The stallholder wrapped the ribbons up and handed each girl her own packet.

The day had started well and, as they walked along, there were stalls selling toffee apples, shoes, riding boots, harnesses and saddles. There were also plenty of food stalls, cheeses from the farms, hams, bacon and sausages. There was a stall selling salt, herbs, spices and vinegars of all types: even the salt was sold in many different ways: large lumps of salt, very fine salt; it was a fine sight to see, especially as most things had been produced there in the county. John looked at Elizabeth and said, 'You are very interested in all of the ingredients,' and Elizabeth replied, 'Yes, I was taught to cook by Mrs Jolly, she explained all the different ingredients and their use in cooking and I like to see all the different ingredients on the stall.'

John said, 'If you are interested in the salt, we have a salt mine and, if you would like, I will take you to the mine and show you how all the salt is graded.'

'I would like that very much,' Elizabeth replied.

They walked along and came across an ox roast; the ox was enormous, the spit ran through the middle of the beast and there were two men each side of the spit, turning a wheel to make sure the ox was cooked evenly. Underneath was a charcoal fire, a huge tray was collecting all the juices and the smell was beautiful. They walked on past and came across a stall selling pies, these were mainly mutton pies as they were the most popular. The two girls marvelled at the sounds of the fair and the sight and tantalising smells of all the foods. John asked, if they would like some refreshments from the food tent, Annabelle and Elizabeth said yes they would, seeing all the food stalls had made them hungry.

John led the way to the food tent, it had long tables and benches and they found a place to sit. A serving maid came to them and asked what they would like. John asked the two girls if they would like roast beef and they both said they would so he asked the maid to fetch them all roast beef with some bread and he would have a light beer and the girls some fresh lemonade.

Within a few minutes, she returned with the food, there were three platters with good slices of beef and fresh bread; she fetched salt, pepper and mustard. They all tucked in to the food with much relish as they all realised how hungry they felt, the food was well presented and tasted delicious. When the meal was finished, John asked Annabelle and Elizabeth if they would like to continue looking around the fair, as there was a lot more to see.

They walked round looking at all the stalls and they came across a stall selling candles, the candle maker was there, selling his wares. There were some candles which were lit and the smell was wonderful. The girls stopped at the stall and the candle maker told them the candles made with beeswax were the best as they smelled nice but the ones made with tallow smelled unpleasant. All the shapes and designs of the candles fascinated Annabelle and Elizabeth, they then moved on to the next stall, which sold honey and sugar. The honey was in big pots, the man told them it was honey made in the county, but the sugar came from the West Indies.

He explained that there are different types of sugar for all different uses, he told them the very black sugar was for making fruitcakes and the lighter sugar for making a lighter cake, then there was another sugar for using in puddings. He told them the black sugar was also used in curing, as sugar is a preservative so farmers use sugar and salt to cure their own bacon from their own pigs. It was like looking at Aladdin's cave, there were so many different varieties of sugar and salt.

At the next stall, was a man roasting chestnuts; the smell was delicious so John asked Annabelle and Elizabeth if they would like to try some. They both said they would. The chestnuts were roasted over charcoal, which gave them a lovely flavour, both girls thought they tasted delicious. The next stall was selling toffee apples: the lady on the stall told John that all young ladies like toffee apples, but both girls declined as they had just eaten the chestnuts.

They walked further on; John asked them if they would like to look at the livestock as everyone from the county had brought their animals to the show to see if they could win any prizes and a rosette for the best animal in the county. They walked along and came to the cattle, they were longhorns and John told them they were the original cattle of the area and used for the ploughing of the fields since Saxon times.

These cattle were a strong breed, taken to America with the settlers who used them to take across the plains, as they were such a hardy breed. The longhorns were a well-established breed, both in England and in America, especially in Texas. Elizabeth thought John was very interesting to listen to and very knowledgeable. He had a deep interest in the animals and the land and had taken the trouble to find out more, this gave Elizabeth great satisfaction.

In the next pen were the Herefordshire cattle, they were beautiful cattle with white faces and red in their coats. Elizabeth asked John, 'What are these cattle here?' and John replied, 'These Hereford cattle have been in the country for many centuries but we do not know the origins of them. We think they came from Wales, when Herefordshire was part of Wales. They are very versatile cattle and are bred mainly for their beef.'

They carried on walking past the pens, he showed Elizabeth the Welsh cattle, black cattle that also went back many centuries, again a very hardy breed which produced good meat and were kept for their milk. John explained that, in parts of Wales, the winters were very hard but these cattle seemed to thrive on the hard weather. He told Annabelle and Elizabeth there were many different breeds of cattle and he felt most people did not appreciate them. They walked along and came to the sheep pens, the shepherds were there with their crooks looking after the sheep. John walked up to one of the shepherds, Elizabeth and Annabelle followed. Elizabeth looked at the sheep and said to the shepherd, 'These are pretty sheep.'

'Yes, they are the long wool sheep for this area and they produce wool for cloth which is exported into Europe. This has given this area a lot of wealth over the centuries and that is reason why there are a lot of grand churches and manor houses here. There are smaller mountain sheep but they give a finer type of wool and there are some Suffolks here and they give a different grade of wool.'

Elizabeth thought to herself, 'Knowledge is a wonderful thing and we should know more about the island we live on and the things that are part of it.' Elizabeth thought to herself what a lovely day they were having, seeing all the animals and all the people around them.

Next, they came to where all the pigs were on show: all different varieties of pigs, black pigs, white pigs, spotted pigs. John told them he was trying to improve his herd of pigs at home and said that when he started, when he was a young man, there were only the local pigs that were very coarse animals.

Each area had their own type of pig and were interbred so the meat they produced was not very good. Now there was a growing demand for better quality meat and pigs were being imported from China and Italy to give a better breeding programme. He told them he was breeding some of these pigs to improve the strain. He said that the reason he was interested in pigs was that you could use every part of the animal including the hides, which were made into high quality saddles and boots. John told them he had some black pigs from China, which he was going to breed with his own pigs to produce a better quality strain.

Elizabeth was fascinated by John's plans and effort in his breeding ideas for the farm, she thought he was a very interesting man and liked to listen to him describing his plans for the future. Elizabeth asked John how he discovered the pigs in China and he told her that he had an agent in Bristol and, when the ships come in from China, there would be some pigs left over from the voyage. When the mariners were in China, they would buy small pigs so they had fresh meat during the voyage, which the crew were fed to keep them fit and healthy.

When they arrived at their destination, sometimes there were pigs left over so the Captain and the crew would sell them off to the highest bidder. By crossing the Chinese pigs with pigs from Italy and his own pigs, and by careful breeding, he had produced better strains of pig. They developed a better formation and grew a little longer and produced a better pig. Elizabeth and Annabelle thought this was all very interesting and John said that, if they liked, they could come to the farm and see the pigs. He had been put in charge of the breeding programme and he ran the estate for his father, he thought they would find it all very interesting.

The afternoon progressed and John thought it was time they left as the coachman would be waiting for them. He asked if the girls had enjoyed their day out and they both said it had been a lovely day, they had enjoyed it very much and thanked him for a nice time. John asked if the following Thursday would be convenient for them to visit the farm and he would show them round as long as Mr Jonathon gave his permission. Annabelle said she would ask her father for his permission but she did not think he would object. They walked back through the fair and the coachman was waiting, he helped Elizabeth into the coach and John helped Annabelle. Elizabeth thought John was a very nice gentleman whose manners were impeccable and what a lovely day out they had had together.

They arrived at Hough Manor and John and the coachman helped the young ladies down from the coach. Annabelle told her father that John had invited them to his farm the following Thursday to show them around his estate and would that be suitable. Mr Jonathon told Annabelle he would be very happy for them to go to the farm. John said Mr Jonathon would be very welcome to visit as well but Mr Jonathon told him he was very happy for the girls to visit Edmond Priory and thought they would all enjoy the day.

Mr Jonathon asked if Edmond had been a monastery and John told him that it had, many years ago. There was one cloister left at Edmond he said and 'when the wind blows, it sounds like the monks singing and we think some of the monks are still there'. They both laughed.

John told them it was not a very big estate but, in the past, the monks had always chosen the best land and close to water. 'It is on the fork of the river, we are never short of water, the land is good and we grow most of the crops there. I told Miss Annabelle and Miss Elizabeth, I have an interest in improving the livestock and the land there, I have already started to improve the pigs.'

Mr Jonathon told him he thought it was very admirable to pass something on to the next generation and it would be worth having; John thanked him for this comment. Mr Jonathon told him the arrangements would be satisfactory for the following Thursday. John said he would send his coachman for the young ladies but Mr Jonathon told him that would not be necessary as his coachman would take the young ladies over to Edmond.

CHAPTER 14

Edmond Priory

Next Thursday quickly arrived; Annabelle and Elizabeth boarded the coach and set off for Edmond Priory. As they approached, they saw the house in the distance; it was a small compact house made with well cut stone, with tall chimneys and with oak and beech trees surrounding it. They rode up the drive and peacocks strutted about the lawns on either side; it was a lovely setting and the monks had chosen well. There was an abundance of mature trees and it looked as if it had been there forever. They pulled up at the front door and the groom came out and assisted the young ladies to get down.

John came out to greet them and welcome them to Edmond Priory, he then ushered them into the hall. The hall had a lovely oak floor, with some very nice furniture and in one corner, there was a suit of armour and, above, all the family flags and emblems. He asked them if they would like to go into the sitting room by the fire and he would send for some tea. One of the maids came in with a tray of tea and cakes and set them down.

John asked the girls if the journey had been comfortable and Elizabeth said yes and then commented that the Priory was in a very nice position and John replied that the monks had chosen well as it was in a very good position. He told them the Priory was not as big as it had been years ago but they had retained many old interesting features. He said he thought they would enjoy going round the Priory, as the monks were good planners and builders. John told them he considered his family were the keepers of the Priory; most of it was still there to be seen.

After they had finished their tea, he said that he would take them first to the farmyard as they had come to see the animals. As they entered the farmyard through great stone arches, John said, 'I would like to show you the pigs first as I am very proud of them and we are making good progress with them.' They went into the piggeries and saw how the monks had laid all the piggeries out in blocks of four.

The first ones they came to were the black pigs. John told them they were the latest addition to the herd and said, 'You can see from the beginning we have the original English pig there, which was long legged, scanty and short bodied, with a large head. As we have bred from the Portuguese, the Spanish and the Chinese pig, we have achieved a longer pig, with shorter legs and a smaller head and we have produced a better pig. In addition, the English pig only produced four or five piglets but, with importing from China and developing a new strain, we are now up to ten and the productivity is excellent. The tenants on the estate who have a small acreage, receive a better income from the pigs as, instead of five piglets, they are now having ten piglets. That obviously improves their incomes as, when the pigs have grown, they can sell them in the markets as well as have food for themselves.'

John told them that on the estate they had never enclosed any of the farms; as it had been an old manor house, the tenants had an allotted amount of land and they had kept it. Other estates had enclosed the village green and the land and then went to Parliament for an enclosure act, but at the Priory, they had left the tenants to farm for themselves as they thought it was the right thing to do.

John then asked the girls if they would like to go and see the grain store, which the monks had built and which was still in operation today. The store was where the grain was kept for the winter-feeding; they had also invested in a new threshing machine, which gave better returns as all the threshing had been done by hand but the new machine cut down on labour, and the labour could then be deployed elsewhere. John told the girls his ambition was to make life easier for the people who worked on the land, as it was a very hard industry. Elizabeth listened to him and thought what a good man: he wanted to improve people's lives, which she thought was excellent.

They walked around the estate and then John asked if they would like to look in the walled garden, both Elizabeth and Annabelle thought that would be a lovely idea. They walked up to two large double doors, John opened the doors and there was about an acre and a half of beautifully laid out garden, the trees all in long lines, the numerous beds surrounded by low growing box hedges planted with all sorts of vegetables, flowers and numerous other plants the girls had never seen before. The garden was immaculate; John told them they made cider from the apples as they had an abundance of apples so there was no need to make beer. Everywhere looked very tidy and Elizabeth and Annabelle were very impressed with how the estate was kept.

After a while, John suggested they should go up to the house and have some lunch; both girls agreed this was a good idea. They strolled through the gardens, through the stables and into the house. As they entered the house, a lady appeared and introduced herself as John's mother; she told them her name was Fennella and welcomed them to her home. Elizabeth and Annabelle said, 'We are very pleased to meet you, Mrs Kemp.'

'No,' she replied, 'My name is Fennella, you are John's

guests and I would prefer that you called me Fennella.' She looked at both girls and said, 'If you would both like to come to dinner one evening, I would enjoy your company and I could introduce you to some of John's friends.'

Elizabeth and Annabelle thought that was a lovely suggestion, she was not only a good host but she was a kind person.

Elizabeth was very comfortable at the Priory and thought what a lovely happy house it was, you can go into houses and know they have been full of happy people and events and that seems to stay in the fabric of the walls.

Fennella told them she thought lunch was ready and so they should go through into the dining room. They walked into the dining room and were faced with the longest table they had ever seen, there were silver candlesticks down the middle of the table and it looked very impressive. The footman helped seat the young ladies and Fennella, they all sat together at one end of the table so they could talk more easily. The meal was pleasant and Fennella told them all the produce was from the estate, Elizabeth was surprised, 'Do you produce everything?'

'Yes,' replied Fennella, 'We have a dairy and produce all our own butter, cheese and cream, all our fruit and vegetables come from the walled garden. We keep pigs, cows to produce our own beef, we have a smoking house to smoke bacon and hams, and we slaughter beef cattle near Christmas so the tenants on the estate have beef for their Christmas meal. We do not eat beef during the summer months: we mainly eat chicken, duck and pork and keep the beef for the winter.' Annabelle thought to herself how well the estate was run and how well the tenants were looked after.

Fennella asked the girls if they were interested in needlework and, if so, she would take them up to the sewing room and show them some of her work. Annabelle and Elizabeth told her they would both be interested so they followed her upstairs to a large room that was full of materials and work in progress. Fennella showed them a dress she was making; the girls looked at the fine embroidery on the dress and marvelled at how clever Fennella was. She replied, 'It is not really clever: if you enjoy doing something, you put a bit of love into it and it makes it enjoyable. I do most of the needlework on my dresses and I spend many hours here in the winter creating dresses and patterns.' Elizabeth and Annabelle both understood how Fennella felt about being creative.

Fennella said, 'I think it is time we went back to John in the sitting room,' so they returned to the room and John was sitting looking into the fire. Fennella looked at him and asked, 'Are you looking at dreams in the fire?' and he replied, 'Only if I can catch them,' and they both laughed.

Elizabeth said to them, 'Thank you both for your hospitality and kindness. I shall remember this day as one of my lovely days.'

Fennella thought that was charming and said, 'You will always be welcome here as a friend of John's and, when we have a dinner party, I would like you both to come, and Mr Jonathon as well.'

Elizabeth asked John if she could look at the portrait he was painting but he answered, 'Most things in life I will grant you but you may not look at the portrait until it is finished.' They all laughed then the footman came in with their cloaks and told them the coach had arrived for the two young ladies. They walked through the hall to the front entrance, Fennella kissed them goodbye and told them they were welcome to come any time. John walked with them to the coach and said that, if it was in order, he would like to give Elizabeth a letter to give to Mr Jonathon on their arrival back at Hough Manor. The girls climbed into the coach and they set off for Hough Manor. They arrived home an hour later; the footman opened the coach door and helped the girls alight.

When they went inside, Jonathon was waiting for them in the hall and he said, 'We have had a message from the George Inn; Mrs Jolly has been taken ill and she would like to see you as soon as possible, Elizabeth. It is too late today to travel to the George as the road is not very good in the day and would be worse at night so I will make arrangements for you to go first thing in the morning.'

Elizabeth gave him the letter from John although she was worrying about her stepmother and what had occurred. Jonathon sat on the settle in the hall and opened the letter; he read that John would like permission to call upon Elizabeth at her convenience. Jonathon showed Elizabeth the letter and said to her, 'I feel that is not my gift to give that permission; that should come from Mrs Jolly and, before he comes visiting here, you must have Mrs Jolly's permission.'

Elizabeth replied, 'I think John is a nice person but I do not feel I am ready for a relationship yet as I have many things in life I would like to do.'

Jonathon replied, 'Yes, I think you are right but I think you have more important things to do immediately. There is the message from the George about Mrs Jolly and I think it would be better to go and see what the situation is there before you make any decisions. You will be able to see her and have a long talk together.' So the situation was left as it was for the moment.

Elizabeth rose early the next morning and Jonathon told her the coach would be ready as soon as she was. The coachman brought the coach to the front door, Elizabeth got in and they left for the George Inn. The journey would take about an hour and a half; the journey seemed very long, as Elizabeth was very anxious to see Mrs Jolly.

They arrived at the George and Elizabeth told the coachman she did not know how long she was going to be but she thought the best thing to do would be to rest the horses and for him to go into the inn and have some refreshments. The coachman agreed and thought that was a good idea so he took the horses and the coach to the stables.

Elizabeth went into the inn and Mr Jolly was waiting to greet her, he gave her a kiss and welcomed her. He told her Mrs Jolly was upstairs in her bedroom waiting for her; Elizabeth went up and knocked on the door but there was no answer, she knocked again and still no answer. She opened the door quietly and saw Mrs Jolly sleeping in her four-poster bed, propped up on pillows. Elizabeth crept in, fetched a chair and sat by the side of the bed until Mrs Jolly woke up. There was a fire in the room and the room was lovely and warm.

When Mrs Jolly opened her eyes and saw Elizabeth sitting by her side, there was such joy on her face as she looked at Elizabeth; she said to her, 'Thank you for coming. I wanted to talk to you.'

Elizabeth looked at her and asked what she wanted to talk to her about.

Mrs Jolly replied, 'There are some things that you should know, because I don't think I am going to be about for much longer.'

Elizabeth gazed at her with tears in her eyes, 'Don't be silly, you are going to be here a long time yet,' but Mrs Jolly replied, 'No, I am worn out and I know my time is short. That is why I have asked you to come as I need to talk to you.' She took

Elizabeth's hand and held it, 'You were a gift from God to me, I have children of my own but I have always regarded you as a gift and I have always looked on you as one of my own. You have brought me an abundance of happiness and I can never repay you for that. I am going to tell you as much as I can.

'The night you came to us was the worst snowstorm in a hundred years, the coach could go no further because of the blizzard. The person who you were with died on the coach, nobody knew who she was, and nobody came to claim you, so we decided to bring you up as our daughter. That was the best decision we have ever made, we do not know if that was your mother you were with as there was nothing to identify you, only the necklace you wore which you still have and that told us nothing. I cannot tell you where you came from or who you are but for me you were God sent.'

Elizabeth became very upset and told Mrs Jolly she was going to be with them for a long time yet, but Mrs Jolly shook her head. Elizabeth sat there, holding Mrs Jolly's hand; the room gradually became cooler so Elizabeth went across to the fire and put some more coal on, she returned to her chair and sat and held Mrs Jolly's hand and said, 'I will come again to see you soon.'

'That will be nice,' Mrs Jolly said, 'But I think you should be making your way back now as the light is beginning to go and you have a long journey back to Hough Manor. Please give Mr Jonathon my kindest regards and thank him for all his kindness to you.' Elizabeth leant over the bed and hugged the only mother she had ever known, knowing in her heart this would be goodbye and the last time they would meet.

She left the room with tears in her eyes, turned at the door and threw a kiss to her. She went down the stairs and Mr Jolly was waiting for her.

'How did you find her?' he asked.

Elizabeth replied, 'She was quite alright, we had a long talk and I was glad to know the things she told me and I feel very comfortable with this knowledge. I shall come to see you again soon.'

Mr Jolly squeezed her hand, 'That will be nice; we will look forward to seeing you again. I will tell the coachman you are ready to return to Hough Manor.'

Elizabeth walked down the steps of the inn to where the coach was waiting for her. The coachman helped her get in and they set off; she wrapped the rug around herself, as the night was getting cold. The journey took over two hours as the road and the light were bad; the coachman apologised for the length of the journey, but Elizabeth was very pleased to get home safely.

When they arrived, the coachman helped her alight and, as she walked into the hall, Mr Jonathon came forward to greet her.

'Shall we go into the sitting room and you can tell me about your day at Mrs Jollys?'

Elizabeth replied, 'Yes, I would like that very much.'

Jonathon went into the sitting room where a fire was lit and the room looked very comfortable. They sat down and he asked, 'Did you see Mrs Jolly and what was your opinion?'

Elizabeth replied, 'I think Mrs Jolly is a very poorly lady. I do hope everything is going to be alright.'

Jonathon looked at her. All he could say was, 'Let us hope for the best and live in hope.'

Elizabeth told him it had been a hard day and she thought she would have an early night, Jonathon agreed with her. He took her hand and said, 'Remember in life, the secret of living a happy life is always to think of the good times and forget the not so nice times and that gives you hope for the future.' He squeezed her hand and wished her goodnight.

Two days later, an ostler from the George arrived and asked for Miss Elizabeth. There was bad news: he told her Mrs Jolly had passed away in the night and the funeral would be on Friday. Elizabeth was distraught as Mrs Jolly was the only mother she had ever known and she felt very alone. Mrs Jolly always gave her a sense of belonging and that had now gone. Elizabeth was grateful to Mr Jonathon for having her at Hough Manor but in life, you only have one mother so Elizabeth had poured all her love into Mrs Jolly and now she felt bereft. Elizabeth made her way to her bedroom, lay on her bed and went to sleep as all the emotion overcame her.

Next morning, Jonathon told her he would accompany her to the funeral. Elizabeth said, 'I would like that very much, that would be very kind, if you would like to go.'

Jonathon replied, 'I would like to go. I owe Mrs Jolly a debt as she allowed you to come to Hough Manor and, in doing so, you have made Annabelle's life much happier, so I will come to the funeral with you on Friday.'

On the day, both Jonathon and Annabelle were waiting in the hall for Elizabeth. Annabelle asked Elizabeth if she would like her to go with her. Elizabeth replied, 'Please don't feel you have to come with me. I can manage and Mr Jonathon will be with me. It will be a difficult time but, with your father accompanying me, I think I will be alright, but thank you for the thought.'

They walked down the hall, the footman opened the door of the carriage, they both got in and set off for the George. It took about an hour and a half and, as they came in sight of the Inn, they could see all the coaches, traps, farm carts and horses. Jonathon said to Elizabeth, 'There is going to be a good attendance, Mrs Jolly was a very popular lady and a lot of people have come to pay their last respects to her. She kept a good inn with good food, clean beds and a warm welcome and people will remember that.'

The coachman drove the coach as near as possible to the entrance, Jonathon told him they would alight there and he was to put the coach around the back of the inn, as there would be more room. There were many people gathered in front of the inn as they made their way up the steps. They went into the large room and Mr Jolly was there, surrounded by many people. It was the first time Elizabeth had seen Mr Jolly without his apron; he was dressed all in black, complete with black tie. He came over to Elizabeth; she put her arms around him and told him she wanted to come.

He said, 'I am so pleased to see you at this sad time.'

There were a great many people and they were already eating and drinking. Mr Jolly had provided all the food and drink as many people had travelled a long way to attend the funeral. As was the way in the country, the refreshments were provided before the funeral took place, as was the custom in those days.

Mr Jolly told Elizabeth if she went into the front parlour, Mrs Jolly was in her coffin. It was a closed coffin, so Elizabeth laid her posy of flowers on top of the coffin and said goodbye to the only mother she had ever known. She went to speak to Mrs Jolly's children and told them it was nice to see them and she was so sorry about their mother. Mr Jolly came over and told them that, as the church was not too far away, they would be walking there, following the cart. Mr Jolly asked Elizabeth too as he wanted her to walk with them behind the coffin. Elizabeth went to speak to Jonathon and he thought it was a fitting thing to do.

They all started to leave the inn, the cart arrived decked

out with flowers, the horse was groomed and shining and had black ribbons in his mane and tail. Six men carried the coffin from the inn and placed it on the cart. As people left the inn, Elizabeth noticed several people had had far too much to drink, the parson being one of them and he was very unsteady on his feet. Elizabeth thought, 'Drinks in, wits out'.

The procession started; it went along the lane, Mr Jolly, the children and Elizabeth walked together. Following them were all the chambermaids, grooms, cooks, ostlers, maids and all the people who knew Mrs Jolly.

They arrived at the church, it was a pretty church and the bell was tolling. The men walked forward and took the coffin inside; there were some flowers on the top, including Elizabeth's posy. Everyone filed into the church, it was small so everyone made room and they all managed to fit inside. The vicar started the ceremony by saying that Mrs Jolly had given her life to the travellers and had made them all welcome and provided good food and clean beds. She made everyone equally welcome and the inn was a place of joy to visit. She would be very much missed by all her family, her husband and all her children and everyone that knew her. Hymns were sung, prayers said, and the service was over.

The six men took their places around the coffin and lifted Mrs Jolly up and proceeded to leave the church to go to the graveyard. Mr Jolly, his children and Elizabeth followed the coffin with the entire congregation following them out to the churchyard. The vicar led the way to the graveside; he went to the head of the grave and said some more prayers and goodbye to Mrs Jolly. He then said, 'Ashes to ashes, dust to dust,' but unfortunately it was a very wet day and the ground was very slippery. As he lifted up his arm to bless the coffin as it was lowered into the ground, he slipped on the mud and fell into the grave on top of the coffin. Everybody was astonished, it was one of those occasions when people did not know whether to laugh or cry.

One of the gravediggers fetched a rope, threw one end down to the vicar, and told him to wrap it round himself and they would pull him up. The men pulled him up and he took his place at the head of the grave again and said, 'We have interred Mrs Jolly into God's keeping,' said a prayer and scuttled off as fast as he could go. The mourners were stunned and did not know quite what to do, Elizabeth went to Mr Jolly and said, 'Mrs Jolly would have thought that very funny.' Mr Jolly agreed with her, he took her arm and they started back to the inn.

The mourners started to walk away and left Mr Jolly with his family and Elizabeth so they made their way back to the inn. When they arrived at the George, most people had left. Elizabeth said to Mr Jolly, 'I think that we should make our way back now as it has been a long day and we have a long journey to make.'

Mr Jolly put his arms round her and said, 'Don't lose touch with us; Mrs Jolly would have liked you keep in touch with us. If ever you want anything, this is the place to come. Remember you will always be loved and thought of so don't leave it too long before you come back to see us.'

Elizabeth put her arms round him, kissed him on his cheek and told him to take care. Jonathon was waiting in the doorway, he came over to Mr Jolly, shook hands with him and said, 'I am sorry for your loss. She was a good lady and she will be sadly missed.'

The coach came round to the front door, Elizabeth and Jonathon got in and they drove off. Jonathon said to Elizabeth, 'It has been an eventful day which both of us will always remember.'

Elizabeth looked and smiled, 'Yes, we will both remember this day.'

The coach carried on its way with both of them lost in their own thoughts. When they arrived back at Hough Manor, there was a welcome fire in the sitting room. Elizabeth sat in the chair, enjoying the warmth and nursing her memories.

Next day came and Jonathon told Elizabeth they had a message from John Kemp who had finished the portrait and was going to bring it for her to see. He wanted her approval and so he would be coming on Thursday, with the portrait. Elizabeth was excited about seeing the portrait and could not wait for Thursday to come.

When the day eventually arrived, Elizabeth was on tenterhooks. John arrived and everyone was waiting for him in the hall as it was quite an occasion. He fetched the portrait, it was covered with a fine cloth, and he asked Jonathon if he could lay it on the hall table. Jonathon told him he could, he undid the picture and told Elizabeth and Annabelle he would hold it up near the window so they could see it better. He held the picture up and the three of them stood gazing at it; John asked them what they thought. Mr Jonathon said, 'A lot of people in life have talent and never use it but I think you have used it and I think it is a wonderful picture.'

Elizabeth said, 'Yes, Rainbow looks beautiful,' and Annabelle agreed with her. John had put his talent to good use.

He turned to Mr Jonathon and said, 'I hope you enjoy the picture and I hope you will hang it where everyone can enjoy it.' Mr Jonathon told him he would.

Elizabeth said, 'Where do you think we could hang it?' Jonathon said he knew just the place, it would hang right there in the hall. He called one of the grooms and they hung the picture immediately as directed by Mr Jonathon.

Everyone thought it was a beautiful picture and it was a great occasion. At the bottom of the picture was an inscription, which read, "Elizabeth with her friend Rainbow."

John told Mr Jonathon his mother would be holding a dinner party at the end of the month and he had brought an invitation for him, Annabelle and Elizabeth. He would be very pleased if they could come and his mother would be very happy, as she liked good company and thought they would enjoy the evening.

They spent the rest of the afternoon in the sitting room, talking about various things. John explained the things he was going to do at Edmond with the animals, Elizabeth was fascinated with the knowledge he had. John talked with great fluency and the words flowed from his mouth, he had a lot of knowledge and Elizabeth thought, if you listen to people who have knowledge then you could learn a lot for yourself. They spent the afternoon by the log fire talking; Elizabeth and Annabelle both enjoyed his company and the afternoon sped by.

Soon John looked out of the window and saw that the light was going and told them he thought he should be making his way home as it was beginning to get dark. His horse was brought from the stables to the mounting block in front of the house, John mounted his horse, thanked them for a lovely afternoon and said he would look forward to seeing them at his mother's dinner party. He then touched his cap and rode off down the drive.

Annabelle and Elizabeth went back into the house where Jonathon was waiting for them. Annabelle asked her father if she could have a new dress for the dinner party. Her father looked at her, 'You may have a new dress for the dinner party but you had better make that two as Elizabeth will need one as well. If you get in touch with the seamstress, she has a month to make the dresses and that should be ample time.'

The day had gone well, the week had brought sadness to the door but sometimes, with sorrow, there comes a little bit of happiness.

CHAPTER 15

A Chance Encounter

A couple of days later the seamstress arrived at the servants' door and the cook sent a message up to Miss Annabelle and Elizabeth to tell them she had was there. Annabelle and Elizabeth went down to see her in the servants' hall. The seamstress told them she had received a message from Mr Jonathon saying there were two young ladies who needed new dresses for a dinner party at Edmond Priory. Annabelle told her that was correct, they were going to the Priory and the seamstress said they would enjoy that as Mrs Fennella always put on a good dinner party; they were nice people and she and Miss Elizabeth would have a good evening. She told the girls she had brought patterns and material; Annabelle told her she thought it would be better if they went up to the nursery so they could look at everything she had brought with her more easily.

They made their way up to the nursery where the seamstress showed them the fabric samples, pointing out that the material was a fine Lancashire weave. She thought the Yorkshire weave would be too heavy; she also had some materials from India, which were very fine and silky. Annabelle picked one up and said she liked the dark blue, she liked that very much and thought it would suit her. Elizabeth chose a paler blue material; once all decisions had been made, the seamstress told them she had a month to make up the dresses but she would be back in a fortnight for the first fitting.

A fortnight went by and the seamstress returned with the dresses. They went up to the nursery and tried them on. Both girls were very pleased with the results and they looked lovely in the dresses. The seamstress told them she would deliver them back within the week so there would be time available if there were any more alterations to be made.

The dresses were returned to Hough Manor within the week and, when Annabelle and Elizabeth tried them on, they fitted perfectly. The seamstress knew her business, she had put a little bit of love into making them and the results were perfect. Both girls were delighted and were looking forward very much to the dinner party and the opportunity to wear their new dresses.

On the day of the dinner party, Jonathon suggested they would need to start early as it was a two-hour drive to Edmond Priory. He said it would be very rude to the hostess to be late so he was making sure they would be on time. He instructed the coachman to make ready the large coach, as plenty of room would be needed to accommodate their dresses.

The coach arrived at six thirty promptly at the front door. Both girls came down the stairs together and Jonathon looked at them and thought what a perfect combination of youth and beauty. They stood in the hall while one of the footmen fetched their cloaks. Jonathon told them they would need their heavy cloaks, as the evening would be cold when they came back. Mr Jonathon put on his cloak and hat and he told the footman he did not know what time they would be back but to keep the fire going in the sitting room, as they would be cold when they arrived home and would need a hot toddy.

The footman told him that would be done, then he escorted them to the coach and helped Annabelle in and then he helped Elizabeth. Finally, Jonathon climbed in and sat down;

he tapped on the roof with his walking stick.

As the coach went through the lanes it started to snow and Jonathon commented that it had been a good idea to bring the large coach with the four horses as, if they got into difficulties, the horses would be able to pull them out. Eventually, he looked out of the window and told them he could see the lights of the Priory. They went down the drive around the circle; there were already one or two coaches there. The braziers lit up the front of the house, it was a good sign for people to see where they were and a kindness to the coachmen as the weather was very cold.

The coach pulled up to the two main doors where there were two footmen waiting; they pulled the step down and opened the door. Annabelle stepped out followed by Elizabeth then Mr Jonathon and the footman welcomed them to the Priory. Jonathon asked the coachman to take the horses out of their shafts when they reached the stables as he told them it would be a long wait and he wanted the horses to be as comfortable as possible. The coachman told him that would be done then he climbed back on the coach and followed the other coaches round to the stables.

The two footmen opened the doors to the Priory and it was a glorious sight within. Flowers, holly and ferns out of the garden decorated the large hallway and looked very impressive; Fennella came forward with Mr Kemp to greet Jonathon and the two girls. Fennella went straight to Annabelle, kissed her on both cheeks, and said it was nice to see her and then did the same with Elizabeth.

Mr Kemp walked forward, shook hands with Jonathon and said, 'Welcome to Edmond Priory. Let's look forward to a lovely evening with good food and good wine,' and they both laughed. The gardener had made sprays of flowers for the girls to wear on their dresses; they were the same as Fennella was wearing and both girls pinned the flowers to their dresses and thought how lovely they looked.

Fennella then asked them to follow her and she would escort them into the sitting room where the rest of the guests were assembled. They all walked into the large sitting room and Fennella introduced them to the other guests who were seated there and told everyone they would be dining soon.

While the guests were all chatting together, one gentleman went to Fennella and asked her to introduce him to Elizabeth. She told him she would and asked him if he knew of Elizabeth and he replied, 'Well, Fennella, life is a very funny thing and you never really know what is going to happen. Elizabeth looks so very much like my sister-in-law Sarah did that I feel I must speak to her.'

Fennella replied and said, 'How very strange but come on, Daniel, I will take you over and introduce you.'

They both walked across the room to where Annabelle and Elizabeth were talking to another lady and Fennella joined the group with Daniel and introduced him.

As Elizabeth turned round, Daniel said, 'Excuse me saying this to you, you are so very much like my sister-in-law that it is quite a shock. I hope you don't think I am being too presumptuous but I must ask, where did the necklace come from that you are wearing?'

Elizabeth replied, 'I do not really know but I have always had it since I was a baby, it has always been with me.'

Daniel looked at her and said, 'I wonder if I could have a word with you in private for a moment or two.'

Fennella thought this was rather strange and asked him if there was a good reason. Daniel replied, 'Yes, I think there is a very good reason and I would like you to come as well as I have something to say that may be very important.'

They walked over to the corner of the room, Fennella holding Elizabeth's arm and Daniel said to Elizabeth, 'I hope you don't mind me asking you a few questions?'

Elizabeth replied, 'This is rather curious but I don't mind at all.'

Daniel took a deep breath and said, 'I don't know how to begin so I will come straight to the point: I think you could be my lost niece.'

Elizabeth looked at him, 'Your lost niece?'

'Yes,' replied Daniel, 'Can you tell me, do you know where you came from and how you came to be here?'

'I was brought up in the George Inn. The innkeeper's wife, Mrs Jolly, fostered me from a small babe as it seems I arrived at the George at night in the depths of a terrible winter and my mother died on the journey, from exposure on the coach. Nobody claimed me afterwards and Mrs Jolly decided not to put me in the orphanage but to bring me up as her own, she was a wonderful mother to me and I will never forget her.'

Daniel looked amazed as he listened to Elizabeth's story, 'There is much that we need to talk about as I truly believe you are my niece; this is a wonderful coincidence meeting you here and it is a chance in a lifetime to find out the truth.'

Elizabeth felt very confused with all the information, 'So you are my uncle?'

Daniel looked at her, 'Yes, I believe I am your uncle. Your name is Elizabeth Torduff and you are my brother's wife's child. The lady who died on the coach was not your mother. Tragically, your mother died in childbirth.'

Jonathon was watching from the other side of the room and saw Elizabeth seemed to be in distress, so he came quickly over to see what the problem was. Elizabeth explained, 'There is no problem but a great shock. It seems, from the things Mr Daniel has said, that I could be his long-lost niece.'

Jonathon repeated, 'His long-lost niece?'

Daniel replied, 'Yes, that is correct. Seventeen years ago, my sister-in-law gave birth to a little girl and, in tragic circumstances, the child was stolen from the family and Cheswardine. It was a very bad winter and we tried to trace her, but the lady who stole her had disappeared, along with some valuable silver. We tried for a very long time but, as the winter was so bad, communications were very difficult. It was not until late spring that the weather improved and, by that time, there was no trace of you or the woman who stole you. All the evidence seemed to disappear; the last information we had was that the child had been put in an orphanage and then taken out and after that there was no sign of her at all.'

The evening went on and the main topic of conversation was, of course, the discovery of Elizabeth from Cheswardine. Jonathon said in his opinion they needed to find as much information as possible; he thought they should have a meeting at Hough Manor to discuss the whole matter. Daniel agreed with this suggestion as he thought all the facts should be thoroughly discussed. He was also eager to contact his mother, Charlotte, as she had never recovered from the baby's disappearance and would want to know as soon as possible. It seemed that God had given them a chance to put everything right.

When the evening ended, Jonathon thanked Fennella and Mr Kemp for a very nice evening and said there had been quite a twist to the evening. He told them he would keep them informed of the outcome. John spoke quietly to Elizabeth and asked her what she thought of the news and she told him she wanted to know the whole story and the truth. He told her he understood, a big door had been opened and who knew what was on the other side.

One by one everyone said their farewells, the coaches came to the door and slowly people left. Soon it was Jonathon and the girls' turn to say goodnight, John came to Elizabeth and told her he would keep in touch to see how the situation resolved itself and bade her goodnight. Daniel told Elizabeth he would arrange for him and his mother to come to Hough Manor for a meeting to see how much of the mystery they could piece together.

Elizabeth, Annabelle and Jonathon got into their coach and they set for Hough Manor. As they journeyed home, Jonathon said to Elizabeth, 'One way or another, in a few days' time, we will know the truth and you will have to be patient until that time. When we know, we can make arrangements accordingly after that.'

They arrived back at Hough Manor, alighted from the coach and made their way into the house. The hour was late and everyone agreed it was time to sleep on the evening's eventful news.

The following day, a messenger came to the Manor from Cheswardine and delivered a letter to Mr Jonathon. The letter requested a meeting on the Thursday to discuss the matter; Daniel and his mother, Charlotte, would be attending and they would like to bring the two Quaker sisters, if that would be satisfactory. Jonathon went into the library and wrote a note to Daniel saying that would be in order; he then gave the letter to the messenger to take back to Cheswardine.

The days went by and, when Thursday came, Elizabeth said she felt very nervous, as she did not know what to expect. It had all been such a shock; finding her uncle and possibly her grandmother and that Cheswardine was her home. Jonathon said, 'Life is very funny and there is nothing for forever. Sometimes the truth can be very strange, but I will do all I can to help you find whether you really are the lost child from Cheswardine.'

Annabelle and Elizabeth were watching from the window, waiting for the coach to arrive; Elizabeth was very curious to see her grandmother if the story was true. Then all of a sudden, the horses appeared at the bottom of the drive and then arrived at the front entrance. Jonathon told the girls it would be courteous to greet them at the front entrance. The coach stopped at the front door where Miss Charlotte was the first to alight, then the two sisters and then Daniel.

Jonathon was waiting in the entrance; he walked forward, shook Miss Charlotte's hand and greeted her, then he shook hands with both sisters. He greeted Daniel, shook hands with him and told him he was very welcome to his home and said, 'I hope we can have a satisfactory meeting,' and Daniel replied he did as well.

They all entered the hall where Elizabeth and Annabelle were waiting nervously. Miss Charlotte walked with a stick as she was rather lame, but that did not detract from her being a very shrewd lady who had known much sadness and happiness in her lifetime. She looked at Elizabeth and said, 'I do think you could be my granddaughter, you favour your mother and I can see her in you, but we must be sure of these things.'

Jonathon said, 'I think we should go into the sitting room and discuss the matter,' so the party went into the sitting room and waited for Miss Charlotte to sit down.

When everyone was seated, Miss Charlotte looked at Elizabeth and said again, 'I really think you could be my granddaughter; you are very like your mother but you have some of the characteristics of the Torduff family too.' She turned to speak to Daniel and said, 'On this matter we must be certain, but', turning back to Elizabeth, 'I remember you being born and to be sure of the situation there is one thing which will prove without any doubt if you are my granddaughter. When you were born, you had a birthmark on your left shoulder; that should verify that you are my granddaughter and that these ladies here are your aunts.'

Miss Charlotte looked at Jonathon, 'I think the two sisters should take Elizabeth into another room and check to see if she has the birthmark.' Jonathon agreed with the idea, as this was the only way to discover the truth.

Elizabeth stood up and asked the two ladies to follow her. She took them up to the nursery and told them she did, in fact, have a birthmark on her left shoulder. Elizabeth undid her dress and showed the ladies the birthmark; they both gasped as they realised Elizabeth was their niece. Her aunts both put their arms around her, shedding tears of relief that after all these years they had found their sister's lost child. 'You have been lost such a long time but we always knew God would give you back to us.'

Elizabeth put her dress back in position and they all walked back to the sitting room, one sister either side of Elizabeth, holding her hand.

As they walked into the sitting room, Charlotte stood up and leant on her stick, 'Has she a birthmark?'

'Yes!' the sisters chorused together.

A look of huge relief crossed Miss Charlotte' face, 'Elizabeth is a Torduff!' Miss Charlotte walked forward and put her arms around her, 'You have been a long time away but you have brought happiness back with you. I knew things would become right, because right always triumphs in the end.'

After seventeen years, she had been found; there is good in this world if you wait long enough.

Daniel said, 'Fate has put you back with your family and it is your decision, Elizabeth, as to what you would like to do now: you can come back to Cheswardine, the decision is yours.'

Jonathon stepped forward and said to Elizabeth, 'It is entirely up to you if you want to go to Cheswardine or stay here at Hough Manor you will be very welcome.'

Annabelle then went to Elizabeth and put her arms around her, 'We have been good friends and we have been as close as sisters. If you decide to go to Cheswardine, I shall miss you but I will never lose touch with you as we have shared a great deal and given each other a lot of happiness.'

Elizabeth replied, 'It has been a very long day for all of us and it has been a long road but it seems it is coming to an end. I think I would like to go back to Cheswardine where I was born. I always believed I belonged here at Hough Manor but it seems my roots are at Cheswardine.'

Daniel looked at her, 'The decision is yours; you will be Mistress of Cheswardine.'

They all sat down, each face registering the emotions of the day, each one thinking what an emotional day it had been but now realising that Elizabeth belonged at Cheswardine. Jonathon looked at them all, 'I think we should leave all this for a few days and then I will bring Elizabeth over to Cheswardine, if that is convenient to you all.'

Miss Charlotte replied, 'That is convenient and I would like to take this opportunity to thank you, Mr Jonathon, for all your kindness to my granddaughter and for looking after her and I wish you all good fortune throughout your life.'

Daniel stood up and shook hands with Jonathon and the two sisters did the same. Miss Charlotte turned to Elizabeth and said, 'We will expect you in two days' time.'

The two days passed very quickly. Jonathon told Elizabeth he had instructed two grooms to take a trunk upstairs to her room so she could pack her belongings ready for the journey. The grooms took the trunk upstairs and Elizabeth started to pack away her gowns and belongings. As she was doing so, Annabelle came into the room. She hugged Elizabeth and said, 'We will never lose touch, will we, Elizabeth? I will come and see you and you can come back and see me.'

Elizabeth hugged her in return and told her they would always keep in touch and would always be friends, 'as we have had many happy times here and no one can take that away from us.' They hugged each other again and Annabelle helped Elizabeth to finish packing.

The grooms came up and fetched the trunk down to the waiting coach. It was loaded onto the back of the coach and secured with straps. Mr Jonathon was in the hall with his top hat and cloak, ready to leave. He looked at Elizabeth and said, 'I want you to take Rainbow with you, I have had him saddled ready to ride, and we will hitch him to the back of the coach. I want you to have him, as you are the only person who can ride him and control him. I want him to go to Cheswardine with you, as he will not be happy here without you so I think sending him with you is the best thing to do.'

Elizabeth turned to Jonathon and kissed him on the cheek,

'Thank you very much. I will always remember you for the gift of Rainbow and especially for all your kindness to me.'

They went down to the entrance and, as soon as Rainbow saw Elizabeth, he lifted his head and snickered at her. She went over and kissed him; she loved Rainbow and the horse loved her and there could not be a better bargain.

They all got into the coach, the coachman shut the door and they were ready for the journey.

They set off for Cheswardine; there had been a frost the night before and it made the countryside look very pretty as they travelled along the lanes. Jonathon looked at Elizabeth, 'You are going to start a new life and you must make the most of it.'

She replied, 'Yes, I shall.'

'But you must come and see us at Hough Manor and not forget us.' Elizabeth reassured Jonathon and Annabelle she would not forget them and she would visit often and they must do the same.

The journey took about an hour and a half for them to reach Cheswardine; Elizabeth looked out to see if she could see the house. It was smaller than Hough Manor but was in a nice position, with trees surrounding it.

As they went down the long drive, the house came into full view and, as they swung round in front of it, they could see that all the servants were waiting outside the house. Miss Charlotte, the two Quaker aunts and Daniel were all waiting for her. One of the maids had a posy of flowers for her, the coachman jumped down, opened the door, put the step down and helped the ladies alight.

Daniel walked across and said to Elizabeth, 'I thought you would like to see the staff and they wanted to welcome you back home.' Elizabeth nodded, overcome by emotion. Daniel took Elizabeth to one of the maids and said, 'This is Polly, she was here when you were born.'

Polly curtsied and said, 'Welcome home.' Elizabeth thanked her and, without a signal from anyone, all the staff started to clap. It is not very often there is a happy ending in life but this was one of them.

Elizabeth went into the hall and gazed around, 'Was this where I was born?'

Miss Charlotte replied, 'Yes, this is where you were born. We have lived here for many centuries but this must be one of the happiest days this house has known.'

They walked through to the sitting room; Daniel told them he had arranged for refreshments after their journey. They sat down and Elizabeth said, 'This is a cosy house,' and Miss Charlotte agreed with her and said, 'I am sure you will have an abundance of happiness here.' One of the footmen brought in a tray of refreshments, which they all enjoyed, as it had been a long day.

After a while, feeling refreshed, Jonathon excused himself and Annabelle as they needed to leave as it was a long way back to Hough Manor. He stood up and thanked Miss Charlotte and Daniel for their hospitality and told them he looked forward to becoming better acquainted with them over time. Elizabeth went with them to the door and thanked them again for all they had done for her over the years. Jonathon hugged her and said, 'It has been a pleasure.' Annabelle and Elizabeth hugged for a long time then they boarded the coach and started the journey back to Hough Manor.

Elizabeth asked one of the grooms if he would take her to Rainbow, as she wanted to make sure he was comfortable and he liked his new home. They walked through the courtyard and there was Rainbow in his new loose box. As soon as he saw her, he snickered and neighed; Elizabeth went over to him and made a fuss of him.

When she walked back to the main house, one of the footmen told her there was a parcel in the hall for her. She went through to the hall and found a large parcel. She took the wrapping off and saw that it was a picture frame. It was her portrait, the one John Kemp had painted and the note attached to the picture said, 'Welcome home.' As days go, this had been one of the happiest days of Elizabeth's life and nobody could take that happiness away.

She walked into the sitting room and Daniel said, 'Well, you are home at last; this is where you belong and this is where we want you to belong.'

Miss Charlotte said, 'When you have settled in, I will come and see you and we will talk about what you would like to do.' Miss Charlotte decided she would leave and go back to Chimneys and let Elizabeth settle in.

Daniel said, 'I have asked the housekeeper to put you in your mother's old room and, over the next few weeks, I will take you around the estate so you will become familiar with your heritage.'

Elizabeth sighed and felt a warm glow of happiness that at last she had found where she belonged.

THE END

Acknowledgements

I am indebted to my wife Ann for all her help, support and hard work in making this book possible. I am dyslexic and Ann transcribed this story from the tape recordings I made.

I would also like to thank Merlin and Karen of Merlin Unwin Books for making publication of this book possible; Margaret Wilson and Joanne Potter and the staff of Merlin Unwin Books for having faith, patience and the vision to make this book a reality.

This book is based on a true story of my ancestors and I always felt the story should be recorded on paper.

Maynard Davies
November 2015